MONTANA MAVERICKS

Welcome to Big Sky Country! Where spirited men and women discover love on the range.

LEGACY OF TENACITY

As the town begins to heal from its scars and scandals, its single cowboys (and cowgirls) are ready for a fresh start. They know that love can grow in the most unexpected places and that down doesn't mean out. So make a wish on a Montana moon for all to be revealed—they've waited for their sweethearts long enough!

A MAVERICK OF CONVENIENCE

Tongues are still wagging about Victoria Woodson's role in the town scandal sixteen years ago. Vicky has done her best to make amends for the foolish thing she did in her youth. Now, though, her unexpected pregnancy has stirred up the gossip mill again. Her best friend's brother-in-law, rancher Archer Callahan, swoops in, proposing a marriage of convenience to shelter her from the storm. But trusting the charismatic cowboy is a tough order for the gun-shy mama-to-be...

Dear Reader,

Thank you so much for selecting *A Maverick of Convenience* for your getting-ready-for-summer read!

A Maverick of Convenience is a marriage-of-convenience story that features Victoria "Vicky" Woodson, a woman with a troubled past, a disgraced family and an uncertain future, and Archer Callahan, a handsome rancher with a habit of falling for women who (he thought) needed to be rescued.

Archer is encouraged to ask Vicky on a date by her best friend. When he meets Vicky in person, he falls hard. And when he finds out that she's moving away from Tenacity, Archer knows he has to find a way to keep Vicky in town to give him time to win her heart.

Vicky plans to move away from Tenacity for a life reboot. She's tired of the black cloud of scandal following her everywhere. It's a surprise when Archer Callahan asks her out on a date, and even more of a surprise when he asks her to marry him. But marrying the rancher allows her to stay in Tenacity with her family and friends, so it's an easy "yes." Can they find a way to turn their marriage of convenience into a marriage of the heart? You will have to read to find out!

Happy reading!

JoAnna

JoAnnaSimsRomance.love

A MAVERICK OF CONVENIENCE

JoAnna Sims

Special thanks and acknowledgment are given to JoAnna Sims for her contribution to the Montana Mavericks: Legacy of Tenacity miniseries.

MIX
Paper | Supporting responsible forestry
FSC® C021394
FSC www.fsc.org

Recycling programs for this product may not exist in your area.

ISBN-13: 978-1-335-54090-4

A Maverick of Convenience

Harlequin Enterprises ULC
22 Adelaide St. West, 41st Floor
Toronto, Ontario M5H 4E3, Canada
www.Harlequin.com

HarperCollins Publishers
Macken House, 39/40 Mayor Street Upper,
Dublin 1, D01 C9W8, Ireland
www.HarperCollins.com

Printed in Lithuania

JoAnna Sims is proud to pen contemporary romance for Harlequin Special Edition. JoAnna's series The Brands of Montana features hardworking characters with hometown values. You are cordially invited to join the Brands of Montana as they wrangle their own happily-ever-afters.

Books by JoAnna Sims

Montana Mavericks: The Trail to Tenacity

The Maverick's Christmas Kiss

Harlequin Special Edition

The Brands of Montana

A Match Made in Montana
High Country Christmas
High Country Baby
Meet Me at the Chapel
Thankful for You
A Wedding to Remember
A Bride for Liam Brand
High Country Cowgirl
The Sergeant's Christmas Mission
Her Second Forever
His Christmas Eve Homecoming
She Dreamed of a Cowboy
The Marine's Christmas Wish
Her Outback Rancher
Big Sky Cowboy
Big Sky Christmas

Visit the Author Profile page
at Harlequin.com for more titles.

Dedicated to horse whisperer and
unrivaled equine veterinarian

Dr. Stephanie Hobbs, DVM

Thank you for the education, microloans,
and commitment to helping us keep our
equine family members healthy and happy

Chapter One

"How do I look?" Victoria Woodson fidgeted with the deep purple knit dress with a long skirt, long sleeves, and a V-neck. She had paired the dress with a vintage cream-colored cotton overlay with bell sleeves and embellished with small, delicate purple flowers that she had been eyeing to try on for several weeks.

"Well." May Bell Carter, owner of the Nothin' New consignment shop and her boss of several years, turned her discerning chocolate-brown eyes on her. "You look just as pretty as a picture."

In addition to the many roles she played as May Bell's only employee, anything from selling garments, taking inventory and stocking shelves to designing and distributing flyers for their seasonal grab-bag sales, Vicky was also in charge of acquisitions. May Bell was spry for seventy-five but driving long distances was no longer possible with her bad hip. For Vicky, it was a chance to escape her hometown of Tenacity, Montana. Hers was a checkered past of a troubled teen, and Vicky thought that perhaps she would never be able to fully repair her reputation with the close community of Tenacity.

Vicky turned back to the full-length mirror and studied her reflection. In that mirror, she saw a twenty-eight-year-old woman who furrowed her brow way too much, leaving two deep lines that seemed to point to her freckle-covered nose. The flowy overskirt made her look, and feel, frumpy.

"I don't know," she said, wiggling her shoulders, tugging and pulling on the material that was, at least, loose around her belly. She had chosen a dress one size too big for that reason—deemphasize areas she didn't want attention to be drawn to. The overskirt just added to the volume of material over her body. It wasn't cute. Then she rolled her shoulders forward and tried to draw in both sides of the V neckline in an attempt to call less attention to her now-full breasts.

"It doesn't look like I thought it would." She turned away from the mirror with a frown. "I'm going to go change. Find something else."

The elder shook her head, making her snow-white ponytail dance. "Now hold on, there, V. W. Bug. Let's not throw the baby out with the bathwater. Sit right over here and I'll put on those finishing touches."

No matter what went wrong in her day, May Bell could make her smile. Vicky sat down on the mustard-yellow velvet chair that May Bell had purchased in an estate sale in Billings, Montana, decades ago. The stuffing had long since flattened but that old yellow chair had an irresistible comfy, homey feel that always made her want to take a nap.

"Now," May Bell said, scanning the large selection of jewelry in the display cabinets. "Let me see. Ah, yes! There you are, my lovely."

From the case, her boss took out a necklace with a large heart-shaped polished agate surrounded by a rope of sterling silver and brought it over to where she was sitting. Vicky held up her thick, auburn hair while May Bell clasped the necklace around her neck. It was a weighty piece of jewelry and so smooth and cool to the touch.

She made to get up and look at the necklace, but her boss asked her to hold on. May Bell returned quickly with a hair clasp that matched the necklace. After the elder drew Vicky's hair back from her face and clasped it at the nape of her neck, May Bell said, “Now, look.”

Back in front of the mirror, Vicky’s eyes went straight to the agate stone. It was incredible, with swirls of deep purple, mauve, white, and amber that nearly matched the color of her hair.

“This is incredible,” Vicky said, running her fingers over the heart-shaped stone. “But I think a heart is sending a message I don’t want to send.”

“Oh, fiddle-faddle, diddle-daddle.” May Bell snorted. “Agate symbolizes strength and courage. That’s you in a nutshell, my dear.”

Vicky turned around to look at the woman who had become so much more than her boss. May Bell was her shoulder to cry on, a listening ear, and a sage counselor whose advice came from years of lived experience.

“I’m going to cancel,” Vicky said with a wishy-washy tone. “I think that’s for the best.”

Her elder put her knotty fingers in her ears. “*La, la, la. La, la, la.* I can’t hear you.”

Vicky took May Bell’s fingers out of her ears. “I’m serious. It’s not the right time.”

Especially since she was keeping a very big secret that she had only shared with her best friend, Cassie Trent. When Cassie’s brother-in-law-to-be, Archer Callahan, had asked Vicky out on a date, she had thought it would be good gristle for the small-town gossipers to chew on while she figured out what to do about her small but steadily growing secret. But now, as the day of the date with the handsome rancher had arrived, she felt clammy all over and jittery, like she had guzzled a gallon of espresso. Her head, and now her body, were telling her that this was a bad idea. She had made plenty of bad decisions, so she felt she could recognize one when faced with it. Red flags were waving like crazy in her mind. For once, shouldn’t she heed them?

May Bell crossed her arms and tilted her head with the look of a disappointed granny in her heavily lidded brown eyes.

"Please don't look at me like that, Miss May Bell."

"What look?"

"Like I've disappointed you."

"I'm disappointed for *you*, my dear. Not for me."

Not expecting that answer, Vicky didn't respond, giving May Bell space to continue.

"You have ended your relationship with that awful, terrible, no-good Louis Stronk."

"Well," Vicky said, "he actually broke up—"

"Never mind that." May Bell waved the comment away with her hand as she continued, "You're single and it's time for you to get out there and mingle. Dinner with a red-blooded, hot-to-trot, Montana rancher like Archer Callahan is the perfect place to start. I tell you, hand on the Bible, if I was ten or twenty years younger and not hopelessly devoted to Emil, my dearly departed husband of fifty-five years, may God rest his soul, I'd consider playing cougar to Archer's young buck."

Not convinced, Vicky spun around and bolted to her phone to send a quick cancelation text to Archer. She grabbed her phone, turned it on, and opened it to Messages.

"Besides, it's too late to cancel now," May Bell called out to her.

Vicky's ears perked up as her fingers stopped typing. "Why's that?"

But she knew. In her heart, she knew, even as she waited with her eyes closed and her heartbeat all revved up.

"Because Mr. Sexy Callahan has arrived. Early."

Thirty-year-old rancher, Archer Callahan, had felt nervous for his date with Victoria Woodson. He had taken a ridiculously long time to find just the right button-down, Western-style shirt in forest green to bring out the green in his eyes. Women had mentioned that was one of his many good features, so it made sense to use that feedback to his advantage with Vicky. New, dark-wash jeans, polished black cowboy boots, a black Stetson, and a silver horseshoe belt buckle he'd won on the rodeo circuit years ago completed his outfit. Perhaps that horseshoe would bring him luck.

"Don't buy her roses," his brother Graham told him. "Cassie says Vicky loves more humble flowers like sunflowers or wildflowers."

Archer stopped in his tracks, stared at the phone in his hand and then, brow furrowed, looked at the roses in his other hand. He felt nervous and he never felt nervous when it came to women. This unusual feeling he was having, and one that he seriously didn't like, had to be coming from Graham and Cassie. He'd never dated a best friend of his brother's significant other and Cassie's nervousness about the date had to be rubbing off on him.

"Don't be too cocky." He heard Cassie's voice in the background. "Vicky likes quiet confidence in a man."

"So, basically, don't be yourself." His brother chuckled before he added, "And remember, brother, Vicky was dead set against her best friend falling in love with a Callahan."

"She's warmed up to you," Cassie said in a slightly defensive tone.

"That's true," Graham agreed. "She's warmed up. But I'm actually kind of shocked she agreed to this."

"You and me both, brother," he muttered, seriously reconsidering the wisdom of this date.

Of course, he'd crossed paths with Vicky Woodson often. Her father had been mayor, and Vicky and her brother, Brent, had always been paraded out like show ponies on holidays and political events. And, of course, they were both connected because of Graham and Cassie. There was one time that they were at a county fair and he'd tried to shake off the other girls hanging around him so he could strike up a conversation with

Vicky. He could still feel the chill from her cold shoulder. In the past, he wasn't in the habit of chasing women who didn't want his attention because he had a line ten-deep of women who *did* want to be with him. So, he had busied himself with the lovely flock of single women at the fair but, he had, tucked away in his heart, something that he didn't even share with his ride-or-die brothers, Cooper, Ash, and Graham: he had a crush on Vicky Woodson. He hoped that time would be kind to him and dissolve the feelings he harbored for Vicky. It hadn't. In fact, time had only intensified those emotions, but whenever they were in the same place at the same time, Vicky was courteous but not inviting. She had been cute when they were teenagers. Now, she was an undeniable beauty. But in her striking dark brown eyes, there was a deep sadness that tugged at his heart and made him want to help her to find her smile again. He had accepted that his affection for Vicky would be unrequited. Until this unexpected opportunity just landed in his lap. And he seized it.

He looked down at his watch, a memento given to him by his grandfather that was always on his wrist. It was too darn late to cancel. And looking at his grandfather's watch, he knew full well that he was, as a Callahan man, about to keep his word.

"You've got one shot," Cassie said loudly. "Don't mess it up, Arch!"

"I'm almost there," Archer said, irritated. "Let me go, brother."

Nobody, not even Cassie, wanted this evening to go well more than he did.

Archer ended the call and held out the flowers to an elderly woman passing by him on the sidewalk.

"Aren't you a sweetheart." The woman took the roses, burying her nose in them with a delighted smile. "Are you sure? They must have cost you a pretty penny."

He smiled at her. "They're yours, if you want them."

The woman reached for his hand, squeezed his fingers, and after a "thank you" went on her way.

Archer stopped a couple doors just shy of Nothin' New and looked at his reflection in the storefront glass one last time before he walked the short distance to where Vicky had agreed to meet him for their early dinner at Castillo's.

A gentleman dressing a mannequin caught him checking out his reflection, grinned at him and gave him a thumbs-up. Then he spotted a sprig of lavender in the man's jacket pocket. An idea came to him. He went inside, asked the older man for the sprig, and the man, understanding what it was like to want to make the best impression on a first date, gave him the sprig of lavender and even found a bit of silk ribbon to tie the stems together. Armed with what he thought would be more in line with Vicky, he moved on. He still was wondering if this date was doomed. Graham and Cassie told him not to be himself. How was that a good way to begin a relationship? This wasn't good advice! He'd gotten the flowers wrong. What else would he get wrong over the course of this long-awaited, never thought to actually happen, date with Miss Woodson. He was still cycling through those thoughts when he found himself in front of Nothin' New. He stopped, looked through the window, past the displays, to Vicky Woodson, as fresh and lovely as a summer's day, and their eyes caught, connected, and then his date gave him a quick wave and a small smile. And that smile, a bit nervous, a bit shy, made him forget all the reasons to doubt himself. It was so odd. How could this be? When he put his hand on the knob and opened the door, it felt as if he was walking into their future, leaving their pasts behind them.

He lifted his hat up in a respectful greeting. "How do, Mrs. Carter?"

"Archer Callahan!" May Bell Carter had her arms open wide. "Come here and give me some sugar."

Vicky held up her finger and mouthed, *I'll be right back.*

Archer's eyes tracked Vicky as she walked to the rear of the shop, out of sight.

May Bell had a shrewd, knowing look on her narrow face. After the hug, she hooked her arm through his and asked, "She's lovely, isn't she?"

He nodded because he'd run dry and his tongue was currently stuck to the roof of his mouth. After he dislodged it, he asked, "Did you put in a good word for me?"

She tilted her head a bit, examined him, and then walked behind a nearby counter.

"I certainly did." May Bell Carter was known in town for her eccentricity, yes, but also for her straight talk. If she said it, she meant it.

"Thank you," he said.

May Bell took out a bolo tie with an agate embellishment. "Do you know what I like about all of the Callahan boys?"

He shook his head, suddenly feeling impatient to begin his date with Vicky.

May Bell, having walked out from behind the counter, stood on her tiptoes, flipped up the collar of his shirt, put the bolo on and then fixed his collar and adjusted the tie. Then she patted him on the chest.

"You come from good, solid stock," she said. "You Callahan boys were raised up right to keep their word."

"Thank you, Mrs. Carter."

May Bell took his slightly sweaty palms into hers as she looked up at him with empathy in her eyes. "Your papa was taken from you so young. Only seven you were. And now we have lost your dear mother too soon."

"Yes, ma'am."

The shop owner put her hand on the very spot on his chest that housed his rapidly beating heart. "What doesn't kill us makes us stronger, Archer. You are stronger than you can ever imagine."

"Thank you," he said. May Bell's words had always held a special, intangible weight in their community.

The elder winked at him, took a couple of tissues and dabbed the sweat off his brow.

"It's hot for this time of year," he said with a quick clear of his throat.

"Not really." She gave him a knowing look. "Do you know what I think of Victoria Woodson?"

He shook his head, a bit intimidated by the fierceness in Mrs. Carter's eyes.

"She's kind and sweet and good. An angel on this earth," she said. "And she *must* be treated as such."

"Yes, ma'am. I surely will."

"My dearly departed Emil, God rest his soul, that man was a gentleman to his core. But don't go thinking that he came out of the box that way. No, sir. Some assembly was required." May Bell winked at him with a grin. "Vicky? It's not advisable to keep a man waiting with a rumble in his belly."

"I'm coming," Vicky called back with the slightest waver in her voice. That waver made him relax. Why? He couldn't say. Perhaps they were both in the same boat, wondering how the two of them came to be at this rather unlikely dinner date.

Then she appeared from around the corner, holding a small clutch purse in her hands, a blush on her porcelain skin. Her face framed by a mane of auburn hair.

"You look—" Archer began and then just stopped.

Vicky looked down, then looked back up. "You, too."

Stiffly, he held out the sprig of lavender. "These are for you."

His dinner date looked both surprised and pleased, taking the sprig from him and smelling it.

"Looky there, Vicky!" May Bell pointed to the sprig of lavender. "He's a good one. A keeper, just like I said. He brought your favorite flower! And it matches your dress perfectly! Now, hand on a Bible, my Emil did not know the first thing about romance. My beloved bought me a vacuum cleaner for our silver anniversary."

That unexpected gift choice made Vicky laugh, and he laughed as well.

May Bell took the sprig from Vicky, pinned it to the younger woman's lapel and stood back.

"Lovely."

Vicky glanced down at the small grouping of flowers, gave a faint quick smile, looked up at him with the most soulful dark brown eyes he had ever looked into and he felt his knees give way. "Thank you."

"You're welcome."

After a short, awkward silence, May Bell said loudly, while tapping her wrist that didn't have a watch on it, "Will you look at the time? I don't want to miss my quilting circle."

"I can take a hint," Archer said to his date.

"It wasn't very subtle." Vicky smiled again, shyly.

"No."

Archer led the way and opened the door for Vicky to walk through.

"You kids have a wonderful time!" May Bell called out.

Just before he stepped out, he gave May Bell a tip of his hat.

On the sidewalk, in the glow of the setting sun, Vicky said with a faint, affectional smile, "She can really make an awkward situation more awkward, can't she?"

"Yeah, buddy. She surely can."

Maybe May Bell was a master matchmaker. She had managed to shift the awkwardness onto herself, instead of them, while giving them a nice icebreaker for the beginning of their date.

"Nice necklace." Archer slowed his pace so Vicky could keep up with him.

"Nice tie."

"Thank you. I believe we have the same stylist."

That made Vicky laugh. "May Bell. God love her."

As they strolled past the man in the storefront window—this time the older gentleman gave him two thumbs-up when he saw Vicky with that sprig of lavender pinned to her lapel—Archer smiled. As they made their way to his truck, he was still smiling. He wanted to hold out his arm for her to take as they'd walked, but he'd known he needed to move real slow with Vicky. He was well aware that she had gone through a recent breakup with Louis Stronk. He knew Louis from as far back as high school, and he'd never liked the guy. He couldn't figure out how Victoria Woodson had managed to get involved with Stronk, a man who was short in both stature and integrity. Cassie had shared that Louis had really been charming in the beginning, making Vicky think that she had a safe place to fall. But, in the end, that "safe place" that Vicky had hoped for turned out to be thickets of chokecherries with tons of thorny twigs.

"Good riddance to bad rubbish," Archer muttered aloud unintentionally.

"Hmm?" Vicky looked over and up at him.

"Nothing," he said quickly, glad they had reached his vehicle. "This is us."

Vicky took in his truck. "It's big."

He smiled at her. "Has to be. It's a workhorse made for ranch life."

He opened the passenger door for her. "Watch that step."

Vicky was rather petite and that running board was higher than he'd ever paid mind to.

"You got it?" he asked her.

Vicky grabbed the handle on the inside of the truck and pulled herself up and onto the seat. He saw the determination on her face and her will to embrace a challenge, however small, on her own.

He closed the door, walked around to the driver's side, swung in behind the wheel, and then started the engine.

"You've got a bird's-eye view up here," Vicky said. "I think I could drive my Subaru right underneath this truck."

That evoked another smile. "Do you like it?"

She looked around from her perch and, after a quick couple of seconds, said, "I actually do."

He shifted into Drive and checked the sideview mirrors. "Are you ready?"

She nodded.

He pulled out on to the road and headed toward Castillo's, a family-run Mexican restaurant that has been—and still is—a town treasure for over thirty years.

"Are you hungry?" he asked.

"Do you know what?" she asked him. "It just occurred to me that I am."

"Well, that's good then. It's darn near sacrilegious to show up at Castillo's without an appetite."

"True," she agreed. "Come to think of it, I don't even remember eating today. I actually think I'm famished."

He winked at her. "Even better."

Vicky's stomach was full of nervous fluttering and some downright grumbling when Archer pulled into the parking lot behind the restaurant and found a spot.

"Hold on," Archer said after he parked. He grabbed his hat, jumped out and took some long strides to her side of the truck to open her door. It was a sweet, old-fashioned courting move that she actually appreciated.

He held out his hand to her and when she slipped her hand into his, she felt an overwhelming sense of safety. Security. It was something that she hadn't had in her life for too long to remember. Archer had the strong hands of a Montana rancher—capable hands. She had a gut feeling that Archer would never let her fall. And after the turmoil of her life, her break-up with Louis, she felt rather alone in the world with only Cassie,

May Bell, and her brother to call her own. Her relationship with her parents was still strained; perhaps it always would be.

Don't overthink it, she thought to herself. She should take May Bell's advice and just enjoy the moment. One date was not tantamount to a marriage proposal.

Once she had come back down to earth from the height of Archer's truck, he offered his elbow, and she took it. And, for a reason that she surely didn't know, it felt natural to be on his arm.

"Archer Callahan!" Pablo Castillo greeted them as they entered the small restaurant full of delicious smells coming from the kitchen, and a rather romantic ambience with candles on the booth tables as the accent lighting.

"Hello, sir." Archer shook the owner's hand. "Looks like we beat the crowd."

"Yes, yes." Pablo nodded. "And it is wonderful to see you, Miss Woodson."

"Thank you," Vicky said. "I feel the same."

She had been avoiding many public places. She had tired of the stares and whispering behind hands. She had never wanted to be famous but she had to believe that her family's infamy in a town scandal was even worse. Yet, with Archer, she could imagine that some of those stares weren't for her anymore. They could be staring at the handsome rancher. That thought made her smile. "Let me take you to our best booth." Pablo grabbed two menus and led the way to a cozy corner. "How is this?"

"Perfect," Archer said, hanging his hat on a hook on the side of the bench seat just for that purpose.

"Yes." Vicky slid into the booth. "It's perfect, thank you."

"Good, good." Pablo nodded and grinned. "Mrs. Castillo will be with you, and she will tell you about thc specials. Such amazing specials!"

They each opened their menus, and so much looked good that it was difficult to even begin to make a choice. Yolanda Castillo arrived with water, a bowl of tortilla chips and salsa and a welcoming smile. Archer asked Vicky if she wanted a drink. She begged off, saying that she was fine with water. Archer said he'd pass as well because he was the driver. Yolanda took their orders and she left them to their own devices with the appetizer. That's when Vicky's stomach actually growled.

Together, they took advantage of the hot and lightly salted homemade tortilla chips and a salsa with a mild amount of zing.

Her first bite of a tortilla chip was so tasty, Vicky closed her eyes with a happy moan. And that made Archer chuckle. She opened her eyes and felt a flush rush up to her cheeks. They put a big dent on the chips and the dip, but she didn't want to ruin her enchiladas.

She pushed the chips and salsa to his side of the table.

"Are you sure?" he asked.

"Yes." She smiled at him. "I don't want to fill up." At that moment, and in a quick flash, Archer had transformed into a young boy who had just won a big, unexpected prize.

Archer didn't ask her twice. He polished off those chips in quick order.

He then sat back with a satisfied look on his face.

"Do you still have room?" she asked him.

He patted his stomach. "I'm just getting started."

How could this man, an acquaintance, make her feel at ease?

She found herself studying him and blushing when he caught her in the act.

Archer drained his drink and then held it up for a busy busboy to see.

Now that the chips and salsa were gone, there was a lull and it seemed that neither of them really knew what to say to the other. She was sitting across from this gorgeous cowboy who had shaggy blond hair, full lips, the strong jawline of the gods, and those green eyes. Oh, the green eyes! A woman could get lost in them. She was finding it awfully challenging to not dive into them like a woman who had nothing to hide. Before she could even open her mouth, almost as if by divine intervention, her phone chirped. She took it out of her purse and looked at it. While she was reading the text from Cassie, demanding details, Archer's phone went off as well.

She quickly texted her bestie, promising details later. Archer quickly tapped out something on his phone, too, and then with a rather irritated expression on his superhandsome face, he asked, "Cassie?"

She nodded, switching her phone to Do Not Disturb. "Graham?"

He frowned. "Yep."

She held up her phone. "Do not disturb."

He tossed his phone unceremoniously on the table. "Do. Not. Disturb."

They both laughed at the action they had just taken.

"I know they talked you into this, but they have to let us at least try to enjoy this."

The busboy had come by to refill their glasses, they thanked him and then, once he was out of earshot, Archer said, "They didn't talk me in to this."

Vicky studied him. "They didn't?"

"No," Archer said definitely. "Cassie suggested it and I liked that suggestion."

Vicky felt curious and somewhat confused. "Not a lot of arm-twisting?"

He took a drink before he said, "None at all. I would have asked you out before, if I'd thought you'd say yes."

There had been times when Archer had approached her at different events over the years, but she had never considered those moments as real interest on his part. From her perspective, he was just a good-time cowboy looking to collect women's hearts. She had never really taken his advances seriously. But now his directness about what seemed like his genuine interest made her feel bad that she had, apparently, misread him. She almost told him that she was sorry for giving him the brush-off, but then he asked, "So, what about you?"

"Me?" she asked with a squeak in her voice.

"Why did you say yes?" He winked at her good-naturedly when he continued, "Was there a lot of arm-twisting?"

"A bit." She smiled as she took a sip of water.

That made Archer laugh—he didn't seem at all surprised or upset about it.

"That doesn't seem to bother you," she said.

"Heck, no. You're here, aren't you?" he said with another wink. "Gives me a chance to charm you."

And that seemed to be the end of that topic. She was grateful that he was moving on without digging until he unearthed the reason she had accepted his invitation after all these years. Yes, she had, in part, accepted the date with Archer, with some encouragement from Cassie and May Bell, to just have some fun with a no-strings-attached cowboy. Her life already had too many attached strings. But, as with most life decisions, nothing was black and white. A good time hadn't been her only motive. Everyone kept their own secrets and so could she.

They had laughed together over the fact that Graham and Cassie's meddling fingers had brought them both to this table, and that seemed to ease the last bit of tension between them. They had been in each other's solar systems, passing by each other but never experiencing that gravitational pull; in truth, she didn't know all that much about Archer besides the fact that he was Graham's brother, he was a rancher, and an incorrigible flirt. In all of those times they had crossed paths, she had never felt the least bit curious about Archer. But now, unexpectedly, she was.

"So. The dinosaur dig," she asked. "Are you obsessed or unimpressed?"

Archer's very lovely lips quirked up. "I'm not sure I fit into either one of those boxes. I love Tenacity and I want to see her boom. You?"

"Obsessed for sure," she said. "My brother, Brent, has been partnered with Barrett junior to get Tenacity on the right track, and part of that is putting our town on the map. Almost everyone loves dinosaurs."

"I respect your brother for that."

"Me, too," she agreed. "But it's not just that. I've been working at the dinosaur center, and I've caught the bug."

Their dinner arrived and Vicky's stomach growled loudly at the delicious scents accompanying the food. She was grateful the noise of the restaurant drowned out the rumble.

"Looks good." Archer raised one eyebrow, essentially asking if she also thought it looked good.

"I've never smelled anything better."

Yolanda left them to enjoy and, on the first bite, Vicky couldn't seem to be able to stop herself from closing her eyes and making a noise of pure pleasure.

When she opened her eyes, Archer was smiling at her. There was a new spark in those green eyes of his—as if he had just discovered something rare and precious. She was too hungry to be embarrassed. This was the best darn food she had eaten in a long time, and she was sitting across the table from a tall drink of Montana cowboy. A more handsome date she had never had, and while she knew that this relationship wouldn't go anywhere—it *couldn't* go anywhere—for once in her life, she was just going to enjoy this moment. Live in the now.

Archer held out his glass to her. She picked up hers.

"Here's to great food." He smiled at her. "And maybe a good first date."

She touched her glass to his, but she didn't echo his sentiment. A first date implied a second date might be in the future. She wasn't so sure the first date had been a good idea, and she was even less sure that a second date should happen. Instead, she said, "To a good time."

"So, dinosaurs." Archer continued with their conversation and Vicky had to admit that this handsome rancher seemed genuinely interested in her interests.

"Yes. Dinosaurs," she said between bites. "I just can't get enough. I've been binge-streaming anything I can find on dinosaur hunters, paleontologists, and *that* has led me to antiquity and pyramids. What about you?"

"There's a heck of a lot to do at Callahan Canyon," he said of his family's ranch. "Animals can't take care of themselves. If we can do it ourselves, we do it. Vet bills are sky-high. Feed has gone way up. There's something always needing to be fixed, replaced, built, mowed or cleaned."

"Even with all that work, you sound like you love it."

"It's the only life I know. It's the only life I want to know," he said. "It was tough being a youngster and losing my dad when I did. Then Mom went four years ago."

"I'm sorry, Archer," she said simply and sincerely. These losses had created a bond between the four Callahan brothers that seemed unbreakable.

"Thank you," her date said. His smile dropped for a moment and then he seemed to rally. "I'm grateful for the family I have—Graham, Cooper, Ash. Better brothers a man could not find. And I feel my parents' spirits on that land."

Vicky could see how much his family and his ranch life meant to him. There was the tiniest twinge of envy that adversity had only served to cement the bond with his brothers. Yes, Brent and she had grown closer, but things were not normal with her parents. Perhaps they never would be.

When she was twelve, her life had seemed rather normal. She'd belonged to a powerful family with a lot of influence, and lived in a grand, stately house on Juniper Road. Her father was the mayor of Tenacity, and her mother was, by all appearances, the perfect wife of a mayor. Always well put together, hair perfectly done, makeup flawless, her mother had a knack for organizing wonderful parties that always had a down-home, Americana theme—red, white, and blue, and homemade apple pie. June Woodson was the master at putting on that public-facing front to cover up the fact that she wasn't the perfect wife, or the perfect mother, and that they certainly weren't the perfect family.

Archer had polished off his main course and drained his third Arnold Palmer.

"I do like music. Helps me work, helps me relax, helps me go to sleep." Then he caught her eye in a way that felt deliberate. "Helped me get ready for a date with a beautiful woman."

Vicky couldn't stop the flattered smile on her face or the red flush on her cheeks. Who wouldn't want to be courted by a man like Archer?

"What kind of music do you like?" she asked, and then shook her head. "No. Let met guess. Country."

Archer looked genuinely offended. "Are you judging this book by its cover, Miss Woodson?"

Now she felt embarrassed for a totally different reason than flattery. "I am so sorry."

Archer went on to say, his hand on his chest, "Don't put me in a box, Vicky."

"I am sorry," she said. "What music do you like, Archer?"

With a charming grin, Archer said, "Country. Mostly."

Chapter Two

Archer had a stomach full of great food and his eyes full of a beautiful woman. Their conversation, rocky at first, had begun to flow naturally and he was fascinated by her. She was unique, quirky, marching to the beat of her own drum, and that convinced him that his interest in Vicky Woodson over the years had been right all along. She was lovely, sweet, funny and he was officially hooked. Could he turn this good first date into a second? He had to admit, it wasn't a done deal.

Yolanda arrived to collect their plates. "Chocolate flan is our dessert of the week."

"Do you want split it?" he asked.

"Yes." His date nodded. "I can't pass that up."

The small restaurant started to fill up with patrons, and Archer could see Vicky visibly shrink—shoulders drooped, head bowed—as she slid to the farthest end of the bench. It seemed pretty clear to him that Vicky was trying to make herself invisible.

"It's been wonderful," Vicky said to him. "But I think I'd better head home."

"Are you okay?" He leaned his forearms on the table. "I thought we were hitting it off."

"We were," she said. "We are."

"Then what's got you spooked, little filly?"

For the first time that evening, Vicky frowned at him, and he was quick enough on his feet to read her body language and act on it. For whatever reason, Vicky was no longer feeling comfortable in Castillo's. And when he took a quick look around, he did catch people looking in their direction for longer than just a quick glance.

"Let's get out of here." He stood up, put on his cowboy hat, and then held his hand out to her so he could help his date up.

Archer canceled the dessert order and paid the bill, then they walked out into the chilly Montana evening air. He silently offered her his arm, and she took it. The short walk to his truck was traveled with not a word spoken. He opened the passenger door, helped her in, and then he headed to the driver's side.

He cranked the engine and tried to figure out the right way to handle his date's three-sixty-degree turn. It felt like they were right back to square one and he sure as heck couldn't figure out why.

On the way to her apartment above Tenacity Grocery, Vicky was so still. So quiet. But then she looked over at him and said in a rather monotone manner, "Cassie must have told you that I'm considering a change."

"She did," he said. "To reset your life."

"Do you know why I want to reset my life?"

"Small town," he said. Of course he knew. Everybody within a fifty-mile radius of Tenacity had heard about the twelve-year-old girl who had hidden the money the town needed to revitalize. There were plenty of folks who pinned the blame on Vicky for the financial ruination of Tenacity. He personally thought it was a bunch of hogwash.

He pulled into a parking spot and turned off the engine. He was surprised that Vicky hadn't already taken off her seat belt and made a mad dash from his truck. But she didn't. Was there a glimmer of hope that he wasn't the only one feeling the connection between them? The chemistry.

"I have grown weary of being stared at. Gossiped about," Vicky said.

He had noticed all of the eyes following them out of the restaurant. Now, having experienced the stares, he couldn't really blame Vicky for wanting to escape Tenacity. Start over. But selfishly, he hoped Vicky stayed. He'd finally gotten a chance to show her the kind of man he had grown up to be. He didn't want it to end before it even got started.

"We had a good time, didn't we?"

Vicky nodded.

"Better than you expected," he added.

That made her smile briefly.

"Let me take you out again."

Vicky looked up at him with a shake of her head and a sincere question in her lovely, dark brown eyes. "Why? You know I'm going to move."

"But you're here now. And, as far as I know, you'll be here tomorrow. So how about it, Miss Woodson? Can I have a second date?"

Vicky was torn and that was a shock to her. Archer seemed to want to be kept in the dark about her reason to accept his request for a date. She was even more surprised that they had really hit it off, even though their lives were so different and their interests pretty far apart. Yet, that hadn't mattered. They had a vibe. They had chemistry. And that was the hardest part of this entire evening. Her reason for accepting this date with Archer had been very strategic. She had a very important mission—to throw some gristle for the town gossips to chew on—and that mission had been accomplished.

It was almost second nature to try to shrink herself when she was out in public, and she had done that at the table. All eyes were still on them as they walked up to the front of the restaurant. Now, the rumor mill could grind on while she figured out her plan to move. When she did move, she wanted it to be in relative secret. One day she would wake up a Tenacity girl and by that evening, she would be a woman full-grown, independent and capable, living her life on her own terms. A real fresh start.

But now that she had actually spent some time with Archer, gotten to know him a little, and realized that his interest in her over the years seemed genuine and she wasn't just a number on a cowboy score card, she felt lousy for accepting the date with a hidden agenda.

"I'm sorry." She reached for his hand and gave it a small squeeze. "I shouldn't have accepted this date."

"Absolutely you should have," Archer said with a furrowed brow. "We had a good time."

"We did," she agreed.

"Then what am I missing here?" He turned his head and caught her gaze.

She looked out the window, a rush of emotions pressing a lump into her throat. In another time, any other time, this would be the beginning of a promising relationship. She would be dishing with Cassie on the couch, sharing a gallon of mint-chocolate-chip with two spoons, because real women only needed spoons, not bowls. She'd be impatiently waiting for the next text, the next phone call, and without a doubt, dreaming of that first kiss. That first touch of their lips that could seal the deal for the rest of their lives. But that was a dream she could not afford to indulge.

"My life is complicated, Archer. You don't need that."

"I'm a man, full grown. I decide what I need and don't need."

"I'm infamous, Archer," she reminded him. "The reason why Tenacity went from 'about to boom' to 'doom and gloom.' Wasn't that one of the headlines? Why don't you care about my reputation when most around here do?"

"First off—" Archer's jaw worked "—I think they all need to take a long, hard look at their own lives before they throw those stones. And second, you were twelve."

"Yes, I was."

"And you did it to keep your family together," he said in a frustrated tone. "That's admirable."

Admirable? She'd never heard that word and her name used synonymously. Not in the last half year, for sure.

"I like you, Vicky," Archer said after a short silence.

She didn't look at him when she said, "I like you."

The rancher had a thread of humor in his voice. "You sound mighty surprised."

Her cheeks flushed as he continued, "I can be an acquired taste."

"You are very nice," she said.

"Thank you," he said. "I've thought you were nice for a very long time."

Vicky felt this heaviness in her body. She had noticed that, over the years, Archer had shown an interest in her. But she had always balked from men who were fighting off women, competing for their time. She supposed she had thought he was too handsome, too charming to take seriously.

Now she realized that Archer wasn't just a pretty face. At any other time in their lives, perhaps this attraction between them could be explored. Not now. It just seemed like it was too late, way too late.

Her life was a mess of knots she had been trying desperately to untangle. Her family held too many secrets. June Woodson's secret? A lover. And in order to run away with that lover, June had stolen thousands of dollars earmarked for the revitalization of Tenacity. And when Vicky had found the money, she'd hidden it, reasoning in her young mind that without money her mother couldn't run away. And she had kept that secret safely guarded for sixteen years. She was grateful for her brother who had stood by her side last year when she'd confessed her role in what had happened. She'd kept the secret for so long, it had felt good to confess. But she was tired of the looks and the stares, particularly now that there was the possibility that some would judge her baby, too.

June, to her credit, had owned up to the crime and would not be prosecuted due to the statute of limitations. After she confessed and the whole truth had come out, Vicky's father had been forced to step down as mayor and his reputation had been tarnished by his role in the cover-up of the theft and using his power to put the blame on Barrett Deroy, Jr., only a teenager at the time. The Deroys had been forced to leave town and change their names. Needless to say, the public-facing perfect family facade her parents had erected to hide the many cracks in their marriage and their many misdeeds had come tumbling down like a house of cards. As a family, they all confessed and offered to do community service. But, their once sterling family reputation was, most likely, tainted forever. She felt the weight of that family betrayal of Tenacity like a beast of burden, yoke around the neck, as she pulled the wagon overflowing with Woodson sins behind her.

Vicky turned her head away from Archer so he could not see the struggle she was having to stop her emotions from erupting. When she thought of the downfall of her family, tears naturally formed, and it had taken practice to push them back down. All that tears did was make folks in Tenacity, who felt sorry for her, pity her more. And for those who blamed her for Tenacity's lack of economic growth, it only made them think she was crying crocodile tears.

Then, the only thing left for her to say was: "Thank you, Archer, for a truly enjoyable date. But, I have to get some rest. Tomorrow is a big day. For the town and for me."

Finally, after sixteen years of guilt and regret, Tenacity was going to start the dinosaur dig and her brother's months of work and dedication to the revitalization of Tenacity would start to pay off.

"Okay," Archer said, and she could hear the disappointment in his tone.

Even though she didn't let it show, her own disappointment matched his.

He walked her to the door that had steps leading up to her apartment. At the door, she thanked him again and climbed the stairs. When she reached the landing, Archer called up to her. "Vicky?"

"Yes?"

"Don't be surprised if I call you."

Her body reacted to that statement even if her brain didn't approve. She wanted him to call her. She did. And that part of her was stronger, in this moment, than her brain insisting that she say absolutely, unequivocally, *No*!

Not knowing how to answer him, she unlocked the door, waved to him, and then walked into her apartment, feeling an odd mixture of elation, exhaustion, giddiness, and disenchantment.

She was attracted to Archer. She was human, after all, and Archer was undeniably handsome and charming. Why hadn't she met him at any other time except now?

Inside her apartment, she turned on the light, dropped her keys in a pottery bowl decorated with hand-painted sunflowers, and locked the door behind her. Her apartment was shabby chic, decorated mostly with knickknacks from Nothin' New and other discount outlets. She loved whimsical lamps and anything tie-dyed. A small curio cabinet was jammed with crystal animals and porcelain dolls given to her by her mother and father over the years. She had found a swing chair with a stand on one of her shopping excursions for May Bell, and it was a perfect fit for her limited space. A small kitchenette table was big enough for wicker chairs. The kitchen itself was tiny, and the appliances were old and white, but she didn't care about that sort of thing. She preferred function and longevity over shiny and new.

Vicky put her leftovers in the fridge before she kicked off her flats and knelt on the squishy purple-velvet love seat to close her blinds. That was when she saw Archer, leaned back against his truck, looking up at the window. She waved at him, and he tipped his hat to her before he got into his truck and, after one last wave, drove off.

"Wow." Vicky dropped back onto the deep cushions of her love seat. For a good while, she just sat there, replaying the date in her mind. Archer was a gentleman at the core. Yes, she had really taken a liking to Graham after spending time with him. Now, she had taken a liking to Archer. A rancher she had basically labeled as shallow and a bit annoying on the rare occasions they found themselves at the same place at the same time.

Vicky curled her legs up beneath her, turned her phone on, and read all of the text messages from Cassie. She couldn't leave her oldest friend in suspense.

"Tell me everything!" Cassie's voice was full of excitement and anticipation when she answered Vicky's call.

Vicky drew a brightly colored knitted throw, a gift from May Bell, over her lap, and settled in for one of their frequent marathon talks.

"Honestly, we hit it off."

"I knew it!" Cassie exclaimed. "I called it!"

Vicky laughed. How could she not? Cassie's excitement had always been her excitement and vice versa.

In that moment, she wanted to just be Vicky Woodson, a girl with a new crush and she didn't want to think about the reason she had accepted the date. Yes, Cassie had encouraged her, as had May Bell. But she had accepted to give herself some space and time to leave Tenacity. It had simply never occurred to her that she would hit it off with Archer. But, she had.

Vicky told her friend all about the date, from his picking her up, to his offering her his arm, right up to the last moment when he'd waited until he'd made sure she was safe in her apartment before leaving.

"He's a romantic," Vicky told her. "I would've never thought that about him."

"The Callahan men have incredibly handsome covers and that's not even the good part. The best part is what they have on the inside."

"I'm sorry, Cassie. I was so wrong about Graham," Vicky said.

"We all get it wrong sometimes." Cassie always wanted to make her feel better. "And, besides, you were the one to step in and go to Graham to tell him that I loved him truly. In the end, you got it right, Vick."

"Thank goodness."

After a pause, Cassie asked, "So, you really like Archer? Like, *really* like him?"

Vicky breathed in, pondered the question before she said, "Yes. I really do. I unexpectedly do. We just…"

"Clicked."

"Yes."

"Then I did the right thing by setting the two of you up."

Of course, Vicky knew that Cassie had put the wheels in motion. But Vicky now believed Archer. He had always been interested, and he decided to throw his hat in the ring and see if she would pick it up. And she had.

"I—" Vicky began, stopped, searched for the right words, and then restarted. "I enjoyed my time with him. I did. But that one date doesn't change anything, Cassie. I still need to leave Tenacity. Start over completely. I have more than just myself to consider now."

There was a pause at the end of the line.

"I don't want you to leave, Vicky."

"I know."

"Maybe a new romance could change your mind," Cassie said. "Look at Graham and me. Who would have guessed how our love story would unfold? I was his fake girlfriend while he ran for mayor. And now it's a real romance and true love."

When anyone talked about the elections for mayor, it always gave Vicky a twinge of hurt in her gut. But lately, she had managed to learn how to forgive her parents for their sins and now, she hoped, that she could begin to forgive herself.

"I'm so glad it worked out for you and Graham, Cass," Vicky said. "But I don't believe that's my path. My path is leading me out of Tenacity. To where, I'm not sure."

Vicky yawned loudly, feeling so tired. "Let's talk more about it later, okay? Tomorrow is a big day, and I want to be rested so I can enjoy it."

The ground had finally thawed, and the town was having its inaugural dinosaur dig. Digging for dinosaurs had been a part of the town revitalization plans before June had stolen the money and Vicky had hidden it. For Vicky, this was more than just a dig—this was life coming full circle. Tenacity, sixteen years later, was going to finally have a claim to fame and a destination for tourists to come and visit. That tourism would bring revenue, and revenue would encourage businesses to open, and that would pull Tenacity out of the near financial ruin. Maybe her leaving was two-fold—a life reboot and she would be far enough from Tenacity not to mess things up again.

"But," Cassie said after a loud yawn, "sleep on this. For once, why not just loosen up and have some fun with a cute cowboy? What could be the harm in that?"

Vicky hung up after promising Cassie to "loosen up," but as for the harm it could do? She could see herself really falling for Archer, and when she had to let him go, it would cause her heart a whole world of harm.

Vicky was up before the crack of dawn. With dinosaurs on their minds, the townspeople were buzzing with excitement, and she shared that excitement and anticipation. She made herself a quick breakfast of scrambled eggs and toast with strawberry preserves, took a shower, watered her many plants, and then donned her signature flowy dress, plus a cardigan to keep her warm until the sun was out in full force, and then and a pair of thick-sole boots. She couldn't resist wearing the agate necklace May Bell had given her yesterday. It made her wonder if Archer, who would undoubtedly be at the dig site, would be wearing that bolo tie.

As if he'd heard her thinking about him, Archer called her. Vicky looked at the phone, shocked and feeling like a deer in the headlights—frozen in her spot.

"Hello?" she asked when she decided to answer the call.

"Mornin'," Archer said in that lovely cowboy drawl that made those butterflies take flight.

"Good morning."

"Did I wake you?"

"No." She laughed. "I was up before dawn."

"You, me, and every other person in Tenacity."

"True." Vicky heard a smile in her voice. She felt like a giddy teenaged girl talking on the phone with her first crush. That didn't change the fact that her life was heading in the opposite direction from Tenacity. Her newfound crush on Archer would make it harder to leave, but leave she would.

"Of course, ranch life gets me up before dawn most days," Archer said. "This morning, while I was taking care of the horses, it gave me time to think about you."

That confession shocked her, and she couldn't find any words to say.

"Did you have time to think about me?" he asked her.

"Flirt." A word finally came to her.

Archer chuckled. "No sense denying that."

Vicky settled into her swinging chair, one leg tucked under the other, one foot gently rocking her back and forth.

"While I was out there in the barn, I came to a conclusion. Do you want to hear it?"

"I'm not sure."

Another chuckle. "I came to the conclusion that I'd like to take you to the inaugural dig."

And that was the second moment of silence he had caused.

In a joking tone, Archer said, "Blink twice if you heard me."

"I heard you," she said. "I just don't know what I should say."

"I'm only taking *yes* for an answer this morning."

Vicky tucked a wayward strand of hair behind her ear. The answer should be *no. No. No. No. No!*

"I do like you, Archer."

"Then we're off to a good start."

"Start and finish," she said, without any sense of pleasure. "I am moving, Archer. Right after I am finished with community service."

This time he had no flirtatious comeback.

"I remember," he said seriously. "But that doesn't scare me. We're just having a bit of fun. You're going to the dig anyway. Why not go with a handsome rancher who makes you laugh?"

"Humble, too, aren't you?"

"Is that a yes?"

"You do make me laugh."

"Well, then, there you go! Laughter is good for your health. Going out on a second date with me is a healthy choice. I'll pick you up at eight."

"Okay."

"Okay?"

"Yes!" she said with a smile. "I'll go with you."

Archer gave a whoop, but as they hung up she shook her head. *Victoria Woodson, what in the world are you doing?*

Archer arrived at Vicky's apartment early, so he took a seat on a nearby bench to cool his heels until he would knock on her door. The sidewalk was already filled with people walking to the site of the dig, located near the new Tenacity Dinosaur Center and Park. The townsfolk were carrying umbrellas, coolers, sunscreen, and picnic baskets. This was the biggest event Tenacity had seen in a long while and the crackling excitement in the air felt good. It felt right. And it felt long overdue. Folks greeted him as they walked by, and he greeted them back.

He looked at his phone, saw that it was time to get Vicky. He went up the steps two at a time and then knocked on her door. Vicky opened the door wearing a cardigan, a sundress, and boots. Her auburn hair was plaited into a thick braid beneath a wide-brimmed straw hat. Her pretty face was scrubbed clean and there was a lovely pink glow on her cheeks. He wanted to believe he had something to do with that glow.

"Hi!" Vicky greeted him with a smile that seemed to be entirely genuine.

"Howdy," he said.

"Nice tie." Vicky saw the bolo first.

"Nice necklace." He noticed her necklace second.

"Do you want to walk or ride?"

"I like to walk."

"So do I."

They joined the slow-moving groups of people on their way to the dig site. Archer was happy to be with Vicky, to escort her. But even though he had gone to sleep thinking about Vicky's sweetness and beauty, he had awakened with a sense of uncertainty. Not enough to keep him away, but enough to make him think. He had not always been lucky in love. Quite the opposite, in reality. He had always faltered because he seemed to gravitate to damsels in distress. Was Vicky Woodson just another damsel he imagined he could save? He wanted to believe he had matured—grown. Was he one hundred percent certain Vicky wasn't another damsel for him to rescue? No. He wasn't. But he was one hundred percent certain that he wanted to know more about the pretty Miss Woodson. Was there any harm in that? Maybe. But he didn't want to focus on that now.

Chapter Three

"I brought water, fruit, and protein bars for us," Vicky said. She was carrying a backpack that also had a sunflower motif.

"You're a good woman," he said.

She smiled at him. A small, rather shy smile that made him feel happy. It made him want to keep right on making her smile. And when she smiled, it drew his attention to those lovely, full lips. Lips that were made for this Callahan man to kiss.

On the way to the dig site, Archer did catch some sidelong looks aimed at Vicky, some whispers behind hands. He didn't like it. He felt protective of Vicky. She'd had a real rough go. Real rough. But should the bad deeds of her family, and the choice she made as a kid, sentence her to a lifetime of negative attention? Pity or blame. He knew, even without Cassie telling him, that the scandal, her role in it, had taken a toll, and this toll had made Vicky want to get away from Tenacity. To escape. But nothing, as far he was concerned, was set in stone.

And damn it. He didn't want her to go, either, just when he was trying to get to know her. He was now on Team Cassie.

"Look at this!" Vicky's blue eyes were shining. "I can't believe this day is finally here!"

There were kids holding dinosaur balloons running through the crowd, a band playing, and face-painters with long lines forming. The scents coming from food trucks filled the air—everything from cotton candy and waffles to hot dogs and burgers. Together, Vicky and Archer wound through the gatherings and managed to make their way over to where Graham and Cassie were standing.

Archer and Graham shook hands as Archer said, “Good to see you, brother. Are Ash and Cooper here?”

“They’re making the rounds,” his eldest brother said.

Cassie’s face registered shock before she hugged her friend and then hugged him. “What are you two doing here together? Please tell me that it’s a second date.”

“Don’t meddle,” Graham said to his fiancée.

“Oh, please,” Cassie said easily. “Vicky and I have a life-long pass on meddling in each other’s lives.”

“We were coming anyway, so why not go together?” Vicky said.

“It’s a second date,” Archer confirmed.

Cassie clapped her hands together. “Yay!”

The conversation between them ended when the new mayor of Tenacity, JenniLynn Garrett, walked up to the microphone. A hush went over the crowd while the mayor prepared to kick off the dinosaur dig.

“I hope we find more bones!” Vicky had her hands clasped together, her face hopeful. Archer sensed that this dig, waylaid for sixteen-odd years, meant more to Vicky than just about anyone in this town.

Mayor Garrett gave her speech, growing into her role as head of the town, and Archer was grateful it wasn’t a long one. The mayor seemed just as anxious as the rest of them to get the dig started in the hope that the town would find dinosaur gold in the form of more bones. The new mayor had given grants to well-respected paleontologists trained in the proper identification of fossils as well as how to excavate the bones. They also came with a large field crew comprised of graduate students participating for college credits and the experience. Any fossils found would have to be properly collected, labeled, and secured for safe travel to a safe room at the dinosaur center. If the fossils turned out to be a nearly intact T. rex, it could bring millions to the town.

Mayor Garrett ended her short speech with a resounding, "Let the digging begin!"

And that sentiment drew loud clapping and cheers from the attendees, including Archer. If they found more bones, Tenacity could be on the way to a more secure financial future. This was his home, and he imagined it always would be. The success of their ranch, the same as the others in this crowd, depended on a strong Tenacity. There was also a reason he wanted bones to be found right away—if bones were found, and the town began to forgive Vicky her deed from sixteen years ago, would she consider staying? He hoped that would be the case. Vicky was someone very special and he wanted to see where their relationship could go. But for that to happen, he needed her to stay in Tenacity.

"Bring on the bones!" he called out with a long whistle. "Fast and lots of 'em!"

It was one of those rare, perfect moments when everyone was happy, excited, full of positive and hopeful energy. That was the feeling at the dig site this morning. Vicky could feel it in her body, the palpable electricity in the crowd, and it helped her transcend any lingering guilt she had carried for sixteen years. The four of them, Cassie, Graham, Archer, and Vicky, found a spot where they could lay down the blanket Cassie had brought and make themselves at home. Feeling relaxed in the moment, the warmth of the morning sun on her face as she tilted her head up, she closed her eyes and breathed a sigh of relief past her lips.

Cassie was sitting to her left, while the brothers sat at the front of the blanket, turned around so they were facing their women. Her best friend put her arm around her, leaned over, and whispered, "Second date. I *knew* the two of you would make a great pair. Now we can double-date!"

"We aren't a pair." Vicky's eyes darted to Archer, who was more interested in her than in the goings-on at the dig. He beamed—and darned if she didn't blush.

If she wasn't so invested in this dinosaur dig, she would have been tempted to excuse herself and head home. Archer Callahan was a complication she didn't need. He was a diversion, yes, and a handsome one at that, but seriously exploring this undeniable chemistry between them was a fool's errand. She hoped all her missteps in life had at least taught her that much.

"They found something!" someone closer to the grandstand yelled.

Every thought of her ill-fated budding romance with Archer took flight. She looked at her companions and asked, "What did he say? They found something?"

A rumbling in the large crowd began to get louder and louder while, one by one, those seated stood and those standing moved forward.

"They found something!" This was a collective chant as all the attendees hugged their friends and family. It felt like Christmas.

"Well, hell. What'd they find? Is it a state secret?" an old-timer called out, his hands tucked into his bib overalls, his faded ballcap snug on his head, and a bushy yellowed beard hanging from his chin.

The mayor returned to the podium and shouted to the crowd, "They found a bone! They found a bone!"

Cassie hugged Vicky. She hugged her so tightly. Her friend knew the importance of this find to Vicky. And Vicky clung to Cassie, holding her firmly as tears of relief couldn't be stopped. Not this time, they couldn't. She could finally unload the burden she had carried for sixteen years.

"Hey." Archer was at her side. "What's wrong? What'd I miss?"

Cassie said, "A wrong has been righted."

Vicky stepped back and wiped her tears away quickly. This time, she wasn't the center of attention, and she felt grateful for it.

Archer, still at Vicky's side, was quiet but concerned. "Do you want to go?"

She shook her head.

While many in the crowd were still cheering, clapping and celebrating the first real win for the town of Tenacity, and what that win could do for the town for years to come, a man walked up the steps of the grandstand, strutted across the stage to the microphone like a rooster in a henhouse, and waved some official-looking documents in the air.

"Who's that?" Cassie asked Graham.

"I've seen him around. I think he was at the Silver Spur," Graham said.

"Yeah. That's right. I think I saw him at the masquerade ball. I can't put my finger on his name, though," Archer agreed.

The man, now flanked by two other men looking completely out of place with navy blue suits, held those documents high up in the air and bellowed, "My name is Bradley Bruckner, and these papers right here prove that I'm the rightful and lawful owner of this land. You're digging on my land and that bone you just found, and any more like it, belong to me!"

Mayor Garrett seemed momentarily stunned, like the rest of the crowd, but she managed to quickly recover and scan the documents while the townsfolk began to boo, hurling a few expletives at Bruckner. The mood, which had been so hopeful and celebratory, had quickly changed to shock, anger, and disappointment.

"That can't be true, can it?" Vicky asked her companions.

"No," Archer said, his jaw tensed. "No. It can't be true. Who are these yokels anyway?"

"I don't know," Graham said. "But we'll run them out on a rail, I guarantee that."

Vicky started to scan the crowd. She had been texting with her brother, Brent, who had loved dinosaurs when he was a kid and whose fascination had been reignited now that he was an adult. When the plan to dig for dinosaurs had been scrapped when they were kids, Brent had been depressed for months. His depression had pained her so much that Vicky had come close to telling him about the money, about their mother's affair, and their father's dishonor in placing blame on a teenage kid. She'd tried convincing herself that Brent would understand and agree that she'd done the right thing saving their family. As dysfunctional as it was, it was the only family they had. But no matter how many times she'd come close to telling Brent, she'd found that she just couldn't. Until other events last year had forced her hand.

"I need to go find Brent," she told her companions.

Cassie and Graham nodded their understanding. Archer fell in beside her while she called Brent's number.

"Hey, sis," Brent answered. "We're to the left of the stage."

Vicky had to plug an ear so she could hear him as the crowd's boos became louder and louder while the mayor read over the surprise documents. "I'm heading your way."

She moved through the people quickly, with Archer at her heels. When she saw her brother, standing next to his beloved Sage, her heart felt broken. Yes, he was a full-grown man, but the desperately sad boy he had been was still a part of him. This mattered to him in a way that went beyond revitalization of Tenacity. His love of dinosaurs had given him safe harbor, a secure place to hide, when conflicts between their parents had bubbled up to a raging boil behind closed doors.

Yet, Vicky knew how important this dig was beyond Brent's

love for dinosaurs, something she now shared with Brent. She also knew Brent's frustration over this unexpected wrench in the machine had everything to do with his tireless work with Barrett Deroy and their foundation focused on the revitalization of Tenacity. Brent's dedication to the town was indisputable.

She wrapped her arms around Brent, holding him tightly. "Are you okay?"

Vicky could feel Brent choke up a bit before he said, "I'm okay, sis. Nothing for you to worry about. Barrett and I will work with the mayor to figure this out."

"I know you will, Brent. But I will always worry about you."

He nodded, kissed her on the top of her head, and said, "I know you will."

It was then that Brent seemed to realize that Archer wasn't passing by. He was with her.

"Hey, Archer." She heard a large dose of "what the heck" in her brother's voice.

Archer held out his hand for Brent to shake and lifted his hat off his head in a respectful greeting. "Sage."

"Archer." Sage greeted him with a smile.

Then there was an odd, awkward moment of silence between the four of them before Brent, temporarily distracted from the dinosaur crisis, said, "I'm sorry. Are you two here together?"

"Well…" Vicky wanted to be swallowed up by the ground beneath her feet. "Not really. I mean we were both coming here so we decided to come at the same time, in the same direction, as it were."

She was still searching for the right thing to say, doing mental gymnastics, while Archer said, "We're together."

Her brother's brow furrowed, as did hers. Sage's eyes widened in surprise.

Brent locked eyes with her. "This is new."

"It's not new. It's nothing really." The minute those words came out of her mouth, she regretted it. She was sinking into quicksand. She couldn't think straight. She knew the right thing to do was to send Archer away. She didn't want to lead him on more than she already had. There was also the problem that she could easily see herself falling for him. That couldn't happen. She just couldn't.

From the corner of her eye, she could see the features of Archer's face harden.

Brent was about to ask something when the mayor turned the microphone back on, gaining everyone's attention. The crowd was still restless, their grumbling and frustration sounding like a swarm of angrily buzzing bees.

"I have had a chance to review this with our counsel, and we have to stop digging."

The crowd erupted at this news. Folks were understandably angry. For years they had been waiting and now, finally, the dig had begun, only to be shut down by a stranger. It was maddening.

"This can't be," Vicky whispered.

Mayor Garrett did her best to calm the crowd and get the attendees—nearly the entire town had showed up—moving forward.

"I promise this isn't going to shut us down. We have a great attorney on staff, and he will be earning his pay this week." The mayor's words coaxed a few chuckles from the crowd. "You're welcome to stay and enjoy the food trucks and have your kids ride on the rides for free! All on me!"

After that, people plodded away from the event venue, looking deflated and sad.

In Vicky's mind, this turn of events had only solidified her decision to move away from Tenacity. She had hoped this dig would right a wrong. Clearly not.

"Let's head out," Brent said to Sage.

To Vicky, he said, "Slow wins the race, Tori. Don't forget it."

Tori was Brent's special nickname for her. And because it was his, it had a way of grounding her, calming her.

"I love you." She hugged her brother.

"I love you," he said in return.

As they all took their leave, she looked at Archer sheepishly. "Sorry about that."

He didn't ask what she was apologizing for. He knew it was the comment she'd made. *It's nothing really.*

"Already forgotten," he said. But she could see that her comment had stung.

"I think I'll head home," she told him. "I have my community service tomorrow at the Dinosaur Center—my penance for hiding that money. I enjoy giving tours and helping in the gift shop. After that, I'm closing for May Bell."

Archer adjusted the hat on his head, tugging the brim down so his eyes were in shadow.

"I think we should head back to Graham and Cassie."

He nodded wordlessly and she could feel him disconnecting from her and oddly, inexplicably, she *felt* it. And even more inexplicably, it hurt. And it hurt her that she had caused him pain.

Archer walked with Vicky as they wound their way over to Cassie and Graham. So many people were already leaving, packing up their picnic items and heading home.

"We were just about to leave," Cassie said. "I texted you."

"I saw it, thank you."

"So, what's next?" Graham asked.

"I'm heading home," Vicky said, packing up her backpack for the walk home. "Busy day tomorrow."

"Me, too," Cassie said. "Take me home, handsome."

This day had turned out to be a downer, no doubt about it. And the most depressing part? Vicky kicking him to the curb like a bad habit in front of her brother. Perhaps it was his ego that was stung by that apparent rejection, but darn it all to heck, he'd never had that happen before. He'd had a lifetime of letting women down gently. Navigating new territory with Victoria Woodson felt foreign to him. He had thought she liked him—she had said as much—but perhaps it should just end there. She was moving, after all. He'd lick his wounds and then find another beauty to distract him.

"Would you walk me home?" Vicky asked him.

He looked down at her sweet face, still youthful and fresh. Archer stuffed his hands into his front pockets and wanted to cut bait and leave. But he just couldn't do it. He was, quite simply, smitten.

"Yes." He slid the backpack off her back and carried it by the top handle.

As they walked in silence, the disappointment the town was feeling added a heaviness to the air. Since most of the townsfolk had been at the event, most of the shops had been closed. No one they met along the way seemed eager to open for the afternoon.

"I was surprised that May Bell didn't come to the dig," he said. "I don't take her as a wallflower."

"Definitely not a wallflower." Vicky smiled. "She is a social butterfly, that is true, but you will not catch May Bell in a big crowd."

He glanced over at her, eagerly waiting for her explanation.

"That is on account of her older brother, Gordon, losing his left pinky toe after being trampled by crazed teenage girls at an Elvis Presley concert."

"You're making that up!"

Vicky looked up at him from beneath her wide-brimmed hat as she crossed her heart. "I promise you—it happened."

Archer got caught in those blue eyes of hers. Her button nose, freckled and adorable. Her full lips, soft skin. And her citrusy sweet smell. The more he looked at her face, the more beautiful she became.

"One time, Gordon pulled off his boot and sock and showed me that spot where his pinky toe should have been."

Archer found himself moving on from the moment with her brother, Brent, and instead focusing on this moment with Vicky. Too soon, they reached her apartment. Archer just wanted more time.

They stopped and she studied him. "Do you want to come up?"

"Up there?" He pointed to her apartment.

She nodded, her examination of him continuing, the expression on her face a blend of curiosity and humor.

"I thought you might be hungry," she added.

"I am."

"Nothing is really open."

"No."

"So, I thought I could make you a grilled cheese? Or a ham sandwich?" She grinned sheepishly. "I'm not much of a cook."

"I like ham," he said. "And cheese. Back at the dig you seemed like you'd had enough of me for one day."

She frowned then and looked regretful. She glanced around for anyone who could hear them. "Can we just talk about that upstairs?" She took out her key and unlocked the door to the stairwell that led to her apartment. She opened the door, then turned back to look at him.

"Okay."

Archer followed her up the narrow stairwell to a small landing that gave entrance to two apartments. Vicky unlocked her door and then he followed her into one of the tiniest apartments he'd ever seen. She took off her hat and hooked it on a rack to the left of the door. He did the same, then stepped inside, nearly bumping his head on the doorjamb; everything was small and short. There was a fan in the center of the living and dining combo that he would have to duck to clear. And a tiny galley kitchen and a narrow hallway that must lead to the bedroom and bathroom.

Vicky stopped short, turned and bumped into him. “Oh! Sorry.”

She withdrew her hands from his chest, as if she had been burned.

“Did you say ham or grilled cheese?” she asked as she took a step back.

“I’m leaning toward grilled cheese.”

“Excellent choice,” she said and spun away.

“Whoa, cowgirl. Come on back here.”

Vicky stopped, spun on that heel again.

“Before you go out of your way cooking up a meal,” he said, “let’s finish our conversation.”

Vicky crossed her arms protectively in front of her body, frowning and her eyebrows drawn together.

“At the dig, I got the impression that you were embarrassed to be seen with me.”

“No!” Vicky exclaimed. “No. I wasn’t embarrassed. Darn it. Why am I always screwing things up.”

He wanted to go to her, comfort her. She seemed to be fighting her demons all of the time.

Vicky breathed in, looked over at the windows, and then turned her eyes back. “I like you, Archer.”

“Well, that’s good then, because I like you.”

“I really enjoyed our date,” she added. “Truly. No regrets.”

“I second that.” He leaned back on his heels a bit. “Sounds good so far.”

“But,” she continued, “I just got out of this relationship with Louis.”

He nodded.

“And I just don’t want to…” She paused and then restarted. “I just don’t want to hurt you. I don’t want you to be a rebound guy. You don’t deserve that.”

"I can take care of myself," he said.

There was a short silence between them before she continued. "I like spending time with you."

"Me, too."

"But all I have to offer right now is..."

"Friendship."

She nodded.

"And a grilled cheese sandwich."

"*And*," she said, "tap water."

She laughed and so did he.

"So," she asked. "Friends?"

He nodded. *For now*, he thought. Neither of them could predict the future. At this moment, they were together, and he was grateful for that.

He sat at the table, one long leg stretched out.

Vicky returned from the kitchen and handed him a plastic glass with a sunflower design. He took it with a "Much obliged."

Then he held up the glass. "I'm sensing a theme."

Vicky laughed good-naturedly and he was glad for her lighter mood. "I know. I can't seem to stop myself no matter how many times I tell myself that I cannot buy another sunflower-themed whatever." Vicky hummed and while the skillet warmed up, filled a watering can—with a sunflower painted on it—and made a loop to check on each plant. Her plants were healthy and flourishing and she talked to them as if they could understand every single word.

"You like to take care of things," he noted, imagining Vicky as a mother, taking care of her family.

She smiled at him with a dreamy sigh. "I do. Plants, animals, people. Did you hear about that Japanese researcher who studied the impact of positive words on water. He would sing to the water, pray, and when the water was frozen and examined under a microscope, the water that received positivity made crystals that were more symmetrical and beautiful."

"No. I haven't heard about that."

"I don't know if that's true, but what if it is? My plants love it when I talk to them."

"You'll be a great mother one day." Archer said it without really giving it much thought, but Vicky froze and a gray tone washed over her face.

"Are you okay?" he asked. She looked as if she might faint.

Vicky swayed a bit but caught herself.

"I'm okay." She sent him a weak grin. "Just hungry. Let me get those sandwiches cooking. How many do you think you'll eat?"

"What's a polite number?"

"There is no polite number. We are only limited by resources."

"Four?"

"Four it is, then. I do love a man with an appetite," Vicky said and then started to hum again. Archer sat back in his too-small-to-be-comfortable chair and realized that he felt at home and content in Vicky's apartment full of happy plants and sunflower designs.

He enjoyed watching Vicky cook and enjoyed listening to her hum. Over the last several years, his heart had felt like it was locked away in a vault. Love wasn't a game he played lightly; at least not anymore. With Vicky, he felt pulled toward her in a way that felt new. More important, he certainly didn't want her to move away just when they had managed to connect. Seemed to him that Cassie and he were on the same side about Vicky's plan to leave Tenacity behind. He'd have to ask Cassie what he could do to stall her departure. It would be mighty difficult to win Vicky's heart if she moved away. Time was of the essence; he needed a plan ASAP!

Chapter Four

Can you talk?

This was the text Vicky received from Cassie. She texted back that she was currently entertaining Archer in her apartment. This, of course, compelled Cassie to send ten different celebratory emojis.

"This is darn good." Archer finished his third grilled-cheese sandwich.

"Not the healthiest choice." Vicky joined him at the table. "But it does remind me of my childhood. The good parts of it."

Archer reached for her hand. "You're a beautiful person, inside and out, Vicky. Everything that's happened only proves that."

She smiled weakly. "You're a good..."

"Friend?"

She gave him a real smile this time. "Yes, friend. Now, eat that last sandwich. I might not have a large repertoire of cooking skills, but I know I make an excellent grilled cheese!"

"You do, for certain. Do you make them often?"

She took a bite of one half of her sandwich, chewing slowly so she had a second or two to decide how to respond. She put her napkin on her plate and just spoke her truth.

"Probably the last time I made a grilled cheese was for my ex. He didn't appreciate them as much as you."

"Yet more proof that he was an idiot." Then his lovely green eyes laser focused on the half sandwich left on her plate. "Are you going to eat that?"

She laughed. She noticed that with him, she did laugh quite often and unexpectedly, and it felt undeniably *wonderful.* What had started as a ruse to throw town gossipers a curve ball had turned into a genuine feeling of connection and attraction to Archer. Lousy timing. That was her signature. Lousy timing.

"Be my guest." She pushed her plate to his side of the table.

She smiled at him, enjoying watching him scarf down her humble creations.

"He isn't all bad," she said softly.

"Who? Louis?"

She nodded. "In the beginning, he was kind, supportive, protective."

She could see easily on Archer's face that he didn't buy it.

"I think," she continued, "that his parents' disapproval was something he couldn't overcome."

Archer had made short work of the last sandwich, wiped off his mouth with the napkin, crumpled it, and dropped it onto his empty plate with a satisfied expression on his face.

"Personally? I never liked the guy," he said. "But you just fed me, so I'm just going to take you at your word about Stronk."

He was right. No sense going down paths that would lead them to nowhere good. When he helped clean up and load the dishwasher, she said, teasingly, "I didn't know how domesticated you are, Archer. Kitchen work?"

"In my house," said the cowboy, "it's not inside work, or outside work. It's just work."

"Coffee?"

"I'm not holding you up?"

The rational part of her brain chimed in to suggest she say yes, but the part of her that reveled in looking at his handsome face won out.

"No," she said. "I'll put on a pot."

Once the coffee machine started its magic cycle, Vicky rejoined Archer, who was busy admiring her swinging chair.

"What's this all about?" he asked.

"It's an egg chair."

"It looks comfortable."

"It is. But I think there's a weight and size limit?"

Archer didn't heed that gently put warning and squeezed his six-foot-three frame into the rather delicate chair. His weight, mostly made up of muscle from a life of ranching, made the egg sag nearly to the floor. Archer's legs were stretched out, boots on the floor, pushing.

He looked up at her. "This is nice."

She raised her eyebrows at him in question. "Really?"

"Yeah. Sure. It's comfortable."

"Really?" she asked again.

His shoulders were wedged into the back part of the chair where it was the narrowest. And because of this design feature, his shoulders were forced into a rolled-forward position, his arms nearly crossed in front of his body.

"You're stuck, aren't you?"

His wonderful lips quirked up into a self-effacing smile.

"Okay." She held out her hands for him to grasp. "Hold on to me."

She pulled, but that only served to move the chair forward and then she was yanked back toward him.

He held on to her gently and she felt cocooned by his arms and the chair around them. For a moment, she just rested her head on his strong chest and inhaled the unique manly scent of him. He bent his head and kissed her tenderly on the cheek.

That jolted her out of the moment and she pulled away. "Help me get up, please!"

With Archer's assistance, she made an awkward and wobbly stand. While she was frowning at him, the connector that allowed the chair to swing snapped and the chair fell. With some wrangling and twisting, he got loose and stood up as well.

Hands at his waist, he looked at the broken chair.

"I'll fix it," he promised.

Vicky shook her head. "You don't need to. It was old. I can find another."

"No. I should have listened to you. I'll fix it or replace it."

After a moment of thought, Vicky said, "I'm tired. You should go."

"Hey." Archer looked at her, but she didn't look back at him. "I'm sorry about the kiss."

"No need to apologize. I've already forgotten about it."

Her words would sting him, undoubtedly, but it was a defense for her. Of course she enjoyed his company—he embodied cowboy appeal with his strong physique, moss-green eyes and a face that was masculine and strong. He was also funny and unexpectedly kind. But none of that mattered. Not now. She just needed him to go. She. Just. Needed. Him. To. *Go!*

He held up his hands. "Please, let me explain—"

"I told you that I'm not looking for a rebound," she said, arms crossed in front of her body.

"I didn't think you were."

"And I'm not looking for a boyfriend."

"Why not?" he said. "If it's a match, it's a match—timing be damned."

She turned to him, face-to-face, eye-to-eye, and said the one thing that would surely get Archer out of her life for good. Even if hurt her to do it. Better they both felt small pain now rather than gut-wrenching pain later.

"Archer, please," she said beseechingly. "Any other time. Any other time, I promise you I would be a 'yes.' I want you to know that."

"Then why not give it a chance?" he asked sincerely. "If you are feeling what I've been feeling, why not give it a shot? Give me one good reason, Vicky. Just one."

"Just one?"

"Yes." The cowboy had his heels dug in. "One."

"I'm pregnant, Archer," she said firmly. "I'm pregnant with Louis's baby."

Archer rarely felt at a loss for words. This was one of those moments. Standing before him was the lovely Victoria Woodson, who had just dropped a bomb. Most likely deliberate and used specifically to send him packing for good. And, at just about any other time in his life, it would have worked. He would have put on his hat and taken his leave.

So, why am I still standing here?

"Did you hear me?" Vicky asked, her eyes flashing with anger.

"Yes."

"Then why are you still here?"

"I was just wondering that same thing. But you know, as a rancher, I've learned to trust my gut. And right now, it's telling me to stay and help you. Is that French roast?"

"What?"

"The coffee," he explained. "Smells like French roast."

Her expression changed to slightly surprised. "It is."

"Would you have a cup with me?"

"I wasn't planning on joining you. I'm trying to lay off the caffeine because…"

"You're pregnant."

Lips pursed, she nodded.

Honestly, Archer should already be in his truck, driving back to the ranch. There was always work to be done and he was playing a bit of hooky with the dig and having lunch with Vicky. But he had also told her the truth—his gut was telling him to stay put, and he followed his gut.

He went back to his chair at the table.

"How do you take it?" Vicky asked him.

"Black."

She returned to the table with a steaming mug of dark roast coffee. He blew on it, then took a swig.

"Hmm. Good. Thank you."

"You're welcome," she said grudgingly.

He put the mug down to let it cool off.

"How far along are you?"

Vicky looked down at the floor.

"Is this why you're moving away?" he asked. Then he answered his own question when Vicky didn't respond. "Of course it is." He continued, "I really like you, Vicky. And if all you have to give is friendship, then why would that be so bad? I know you have Cassie and Brent. And May Bell. I'm one more."

She looked up. "You still want to be my friend?"

"Of course. Do you?"

She gave a one-shoulder shrug.

Archer drank the coffee, letting it burn his throat on the way down, before he got to his feet.

"I'm afraid I've taken too much of your time." He walked the short distance to the front door, put on his cowboy hat. "Thank you for lunch."

Vicky stood and his eyes just naturally went to her belly. There he could see the outline of a small baby bump. When he hadn't known it was there, he hadn't noticed it. But he also knew she couldn't hide it for much longer.

Vicky joined him at the door. "Thank you for taking me to the dig."

He nodded, tipped the front part of his hat brim to her politely.

"I'll be seeing you," he said.

Her response? "Goodbye, Archer."

* * *

Vicky shut the door behind Archer, stunned. Only one person beyond her OBGYN and the father knew about her baby, and that was Cassie.

She sat down heavily on the love seat, ran her fingers over her belly, and talked as she always did when she was alone, to her ever-growing baby she had named Riley. She had opted to be surprised by the gender when she gave birth, but Riley would work on a boy or a girl. Only the middle names would be relevant to the gender: Riley Cassandra for a girl and Riley Brent for a boy.

"What was I thinking, Riley?" Now she had to put Archer on the short list of people who knew she was having a child. She had taken a gamble, yes. She'd thought the news of her baby would've sent him running for the hills. But it hadn't. Instead, he'd stuck around and had a cup of coffee, for crying out loud. So, she had told him her secret, and now she had to worry what he would do with that information.

"Don't worry, precious," she said to her child. "I promise you that I will always put you first. You don't deserve to be treated badly, ostracized, pitied or rejected because of who your grandparents are or who your mother is. That's why we're moving. I will not let you pay for your family's sins."

Vicky closed her eyes. She had run out of tears years ago. Even when she should cry, she couldn't. After several moments of calm, she texted Cassie.

Can you come over?

Cassie responded.

Of course! Be there in a bit.

While she waited for Cassie, she pulled down her bedroom

window blinds and then crawled beneath the covers. She dozed off, her move on her mind. The sooner, the better.

Vicky was a bit disoriented when she heard her name spoken and felt the weight of a body on the edge of her bed.

"Vicky," Cassie called.

She opened her eyes to see Cassie's face, and she immediately felt better. She reached out her hand for Cassie's. "Thank you for coming."

"Of course," Cassie said. "What's wrong? What happened?"

Vicky pushed herself up. "I invited Archer over for lunch."

Cassie said, "That's wonderful, Vick."

"I know you are hoping that maybe if Archer and I fall in love, I won't leave."

"Would that be so bad?" her friend asked with audible hurt in her voice. "We always talked about getting married and raising our kids together."

"I know we did. But it didn't work out that way. I have a child I have to protect."

"Graham and I think Archer genuinely likes you," Cassie said.

Vicky picked on a loose thread on her blanket. "I know he likes me. And I like him. That's why I told him that I was pregnant. To scare him off."

"Oh," her best friend said, deflated. She had been holding out hope that a Hail Mary romance would change the course of events leading up to Vicky's moving away from Tenacity.

"Don't worry," Vicky said with a good dose of annoyance. "It didn't work."

Now it was Cassie's turn to be shocked and that shock kept her unusually silent. Then she asked, "Do you have any mint-chocolate-chip in the freezer?"

That lightened the mood and made Vicky smile. "You know I do."

Cassie stopped and pointed to the broken egg chair. "What happened here?"

"Oh!" Vicky smiled with a small laugh. "Archer got stuck in it."

That made her friend laugh, too. "Callahan men. They never lose their boyishness completely."

Vicky nodded but kept the memory of the kiss to herself. That kiss wasn't important and would only cause more confusion for everyone. Their chemistry was absolutely real. But the baby she had growing inside of her was real, too, and that baby had to be number one. So, there could be no more dates.

Thank God for Cassie. No matter what challenges life left at her door, having a best friend like Cassie was an elixir for what ailed her.

Together they grabbed two spoons, cracked open a new gallon of mint-chocolate-chip, and indulged in the ritual that had begun in their youth—sitting on the love seat with the gallon of ice cream in between them.

"Mmm-mmm." Cassie closed her eyes to savor that first bite of their most fave ice cream.

"I know," Vicky agreed, going back in for another heaping spoonful.

"I think mint-chocolate-chip ice cream could bring peace to the world."

"Leaders of warring countries sit down with a gallon of it and world peace is achieved." Vicky laughed.

For a while, they bantered easily, as they always could. But then, real life crept in. She put her hand on her belly. That had to trump everyone's wishes. Even Cassie's.

"You're still so tiny," Cassie observed.

"Four months." Vicky had her free hand on her belly. "I won't be able to hide it forever."

"So." Her friend stopped eating. "When will you move? Where?"

"I have an appointment this weekend with a Realtor in Bronco." Bronco was a nearby town, about a ninety-minute drive. She had been taking secret trips to Bronco because that was where her OBGYN was located. It was a new practice in Bronco and she really felt comfortable with her doctor. There was no way to keep her secret with a Tenacity doctor.

Cassie dropped her head, and Vicky knew she was fighting tears. She wished there was something she could do to ease that pain for her friend, but she couldn't.

"Lots of women have babies on their own, Vick. I still don't understand why you have to leave."

"Too many people in this town blame me for Tenacity's economic troubles. And if they don't blame me, they blame my parents. My child is innocent, and I can't have my baby pay a price for having grandparents who have fallen from grace. People are cruel. Kids are cruel."

"Are you done with this?" Cassie asked about the ice cream.

Vicky nodded. The air of fun had been sucked out of the room. Cassie returned to the love seat, took Vicky's hands in hers and said, "I may not like it, but I have to support your decision."

"Thank you."

"Of course," her friend said. "That's my niece or nephew in there."

"I'm positive that this baby will have the best of the two of us. I hope our baby has Louis's brilliant science and mathematics mind. And my love for all of God's little creatures and my green thumb."

"Louis is a real jerk."

Vicky couldn't deny it. Louis was certainly capable of being a jerk and, after the initial hurt and feeling of rejection, she was glad that Louis didn't want to be a part of their baby's life. Their relationship had been so short, so filled with unhappiness, and his parents had been horrified that their son was dating her at all. They made her feel unwelcome and out of place at the Stronk ranch. In her mind, a clean break would be best for everyone involved, especially her unborn child.

"Tell me about Archer," Cassie said, and then added, "I promise I'm not pushing for that relationship. Okay? I'm just curious. You said he wasn't spooked by the bundle of joy?"

"No. He wasn't. Not a bit. You know him fairly well. Are you surprised by that?"

"*Surprised* isn't a strong enough word. Archer is like a giant playful puppy. Lots of fun, loving life, nothing serious."

"I thought so, too. That's why I told him."

"What did he say? Did he ask you anything?"

Vicky tucked her legs up beneath her. "He asked how far along I was."

Cassie looked down, shaking her head at that tidbit of information. "Odd."

"Out of character?"

"Totally."

"Well, I don't think it matters much," Vicky said, cradling her belly lovingly with her hands.

"Why?"

"Because," Vicky said resolutely, "I gave him an easy out and once he thinks about it, I have no doubt he'll take advantage of it."

"Did you know she was pregnant?" Archer asked with an accusatory tone, while using his drill to take out windows in one of the older barns so they could replace them.

"No." Graham was cutting a board that would make the new frame for the windows. In the last rainstorm several had leaked. "I sure as heck didn't."

"I would've thought that Cassie would've told you."

Graham cracked a smirk. "You think there's only a bro code? There's a girl code, man, and it's strong."

Archer was still mulling his day with Vicky Woodson over and over in his mind. In fact, Vicky was just about the only thing he could think about. She had taken his peace of mind away from him, and truth be told, he resented it. Here, she'd gotten him to like her and then she'd shoved him out the door, both literally and figuratively.

"Well," Graham said, "better that you found out now."

This summation didn't sit well with Archer. He stopped working and looked at his brother. "Why do you say that?"

Graham stopped the saw, wiped sweat from his brow, and then said, "Because she's pregnant, Archer. Are you really ready to be a step-father?" Graham asked. "Look, I like Vicky. Yes, she didn't want Cassie to have anything to do with me in the beginning, but in the end, she was the one to patch things up between us. That went a long way in my book. She deserves happiness, and so do you."

Graham paused to take a long draw of water. "I don't want to have to bring this up..."

"Then don't." Archer knew exactly where his eldest brother was going with this. "It's ancient history."

His brother shook his head. "The four of us—you, me, Cooper, and Ash. We have to be there for each other, and we have to be honest with each other."

"Of course we do," Archer said. "But I don't need to have my past mistakes thrown up in my face."

"I'm not," Graham said. "I'm telling you to watch your step. We all repeat patterns."

"I hear you, Graham. I do. And I understand where you're coming from. I've questioned myself about Vicky more than a time or two. Could I be walking straight into heartbreak?"

"And what did you tell yourself?"

"Nothing ventured, nothing gained. Vicky isn't like any woman in my past, Graham. I've got a special feeling for her. I really do."

Graham looked down at the toe of his boot, his brow furrowed before he looked back up. "You're my brother and you seemed dead set about asking Vicky out on a date, and Cassie was egging you on. I figured it would be one and done. No real harm. But a baby, Archer? That's hard. Under the best of circumstances, babies, once they're here, they are all-encompassing. As they should be."

Of course, Graham was right. A baby *was* an unknown variable and not one he would consider after date number two. So, why hadn't it scared him straight? Why wasn't he feeling like he'd dodged a bullet? He didn't know and he didn't even really know if he wanted to find out. And, Vicky had given him an out. They could be friends, and that would leave him able to not repeat his previous mistakes and move right along instead to the next pretty woman with a button nose, flowing auburn hair, a dusting of freckles on her cheeks, with compelling hooded brown eyes. And those lips! *Let's face it, Arch*, he thought, *you've got it bad for Vicky Woodson.*

Graham and he hugged it out and the conversation around Vicky ended with his brother saying, "No matter what, I've got your back."

"And I've got yours."

After the job of fixing the barn windows was done, Archer went back to his place, stripped off his second round of sweat-drenched clothes, took his second shower of the day, and laid flat on his bed, cooling off, pillow over his face to drown out the light. He did his darnedest to *stop* thinking about Vicky, and he'd managed to fight those thoughts for a good five minutes or so…and then they went right back to her.

Still, Archer was close to dozing off when his phone chimed. He groaned, rolled over and picked it up, the pillow still over his head.

"What?" he grumbled.

There was a pause and then he heard Vicky's voice. "Archer?"

Archer threw the pillow off his face and sat upright. “Vicky?”

“Am I catching you at a bad time?”

“No.”

Another long pause and Archer began to wonder if they were just going to listen to each other breathe.

“I probably shouldn’t be calling. You must think I’m a hot mess.”

“You *should* be calling me,” he said. “And what I think about you is that you are a really nice, sweet, interesting woman going through a lot right now.”

“Well, that’s kind of you to say,” Vicky said in a soft, reflective tone. “I’d feel better if you would accept my apology.”

“Then I accept. What are you apologizing for exactly?”

That made Vicky laugh, and her laugh made him smile. He enjoyed making her laugh; he enjoyed seeing the look of sadness, always lurking in the depths of her piercing blue eyes, be replaced with lightheartedness and mirth.

“I feel like I’ve been giving you mixed signals, and that’s horrible. I’m not usually that way.”

“Hey.” He could hear the self-recrimination, confusion, and naked, raw emotion in her voice. “I’m good. You don’t have to worry about me. Your life has been turned upside down. Anyone with the kind of pressure you’re under would be understandably…”

“Off-kilter?”

“You’re not that. You’re making the best out of less-than-ideal circumstances.”

“That’s the kindest way anyone has ever put the challenges of my life.”

“You deserve all the kindness in the world, Vicky.”

“Thank you.”

There was a brief moment of silence and Archer decided to take a chance on seeing Vicky again. “What are you doing this weekend?”

"Ummm..." She dragged the word out slowly, as if she didn't want to share her plans. "I'm going to Bronco."

"What's in Bronco?"

"Maybe my apartment," she told him. "I have an appointment at noon on Saturday with my Realtor."

It was a punch to the gut. But he wasn't ready to admit defeat. "Care for some company? I'll drive you."

Chapter Five

On Saturday, Vicky was up before sunrise with buyer's remorse. While her community service and work at Nothin' New had kept her mind occupied over the last couple of days, now, with too much time for her thoughts, she was positively sure letting Archer drive her to Bronco was a really bad idea. And yet she didn't want to cancel. She was torn. Plain and simple. Torn.

She watered her plants, ate a piece of toast with jam, and then put headphones on her belly so the baby could learn to love instrumental music. She hoped it soothed her baby as it surely soothed her. When the clock read eight, Vicky called Cassie.

"Don't cancel on the poor guy, Vicky." Cassie yawned loudly. "Have a heart."

"I'm not going to cancel," she said. "But I probably should. I tossed him back into the pond, and then I threw out my line, hooked him and reeled him right back in."

"Don't waste your time worrying about Archer. Callahan men are designed to take care of themselves and anyone they love."

"That's what Archer said."

Cassie cleared the sleep from her throat. "You reeled him back in because you like him."

"I really do."

"He makes you laugh."

"All of the time."

"So, you feel good when you're with him."

"I do."

"That's your answer, Vicky. He makes you feel good. What's so wrong with that?"

Other than horrible timing, Archer was everything she had hoped for whenever she fantasized about her future husband. Tall, handsome, kind, funny. Archer fit that bill with one exception. He was a rancher. And even though she loved going to her brother's ranch and helping with the chickens and goats it was a hard life, with no set hours. Archer could be moving cattle and be gone for days, only to deposit a giant pile of sweat-soaked clothing in the mud room to be washed. The bugs, the manure, the creatures making odd noises in the middle of the night didn't appeal to her. It could also be lonely, surrounded by trees and animals. Much like a grandparent with their grandkids who passed them back to the parents after loading them up with sugar, she was happy to leave Brent with the full responsibility for the chickens and goats while she went back to her tiny, but easy to clean in a snap, apartment.

But the fact that Archer was a rancher wasn't the top issue on the list. At the top of that list was her baby and her plan to leave Tenacity. She didn't want to stay in her hometown, and Archer had already told her that he would never leave Tenacity.

"Look," Cassie said in her no-nonsense tone when she thought that Vicky was being a pain and overthinking every single detail of her life. "When you laugh, your brain releases endorphins, dopamine, and serotonin. It also reduces stress and heart rate."

"Wikipedia?"

"Yep."

"My point is," Cassie added, "you should think of this as a very good idea for your baby. What affects you affects the bambino or bambina."

"I can't argue with that, can I?"

"Nope. Now go and have a good time. Oh! And please hate

all of the apartments, realize your only true home is Tenacity, and then give up on the idea of moving. I'm going back to bed. Love you."

"I love you."

Archer had been impatiently waiting to take Vicky to Bronco. Was this counterintuitive? Was he working against his own wishes? No, not at all. As long as he was spending time with Vicky, he had a chance of keeping her in Tenacity.

He pulled up in front of Vicky's apartment. He looked up and saw her in the window. She waved at him and then came down a few moments later.

He hopped out, rounded the front of the truck, and was standing with the passenger door open.

"Hi," she said, with an unmistakable sparkle in her pretty eyes. Despite the fact they'd both insisted on being friends, she clearly felt the attraction between them, the same as he did. Though now he understood why she was fighting with herself over their chemistry. She was going to be a mother, and she was making every single decision with caution, trying to give her child the best possible life. He admired her for that.

"Your chariot." He helped her climb into the cab.

After he saw her safely into his truck, he got back into the driver's seat quickly, making sure she didn't change her mind at the last minute.

"Ready?" he asked as he pushed the button to start the engine.

She nodded and he could see, so plainly, how beautiful Vicky was with her face framed by thick auburn hair. She hadn't just thrown herself together—she was wearing a little bit of mascara and pink gloss on her luscious lips. Her gauzy, summery dress was working to hide that baby bump, but now that he knew she was with child, her rounding belly drew his attention. He felt oddly connected to the baby Vicky was carrying. Why? He didn't know. He just *did.*

He pulled out onto the road and headed for Bronco. He and Vicky didn't lack for things to talk about. His first music choice was country and hers was Sarah McLachlan, but they had managed to meet in the middle with a mutual love of electronic dance music. When they turned off the music, everything on the list of conversation topics steered way clear of any possible land mines, including Stronk's role in her life and his baby's life, her parents' disgrace and her role in the town scandal. They were just two new friends sharing a ride to Bronco.

They reached the outskirts of Bronco and Archer took an exit that led to an old-time gas station with a greasy spoon, aptly named Get Gas & Go.

He looked over at Vicky to gauge her reaction and the smile on her face—boy, how he loved her smile—let him know he had made the right decision. Vicky was a good sport.

He found a free spot easily, since they were the only ones there.

Vicky took the place in, head tilted a bit, a somewhat concerned look on her face.

"You've eaten here before?"

"Plenty."

"And you've obviously lived because here you are."

"You'll like it," he said. "Once you get past the look of the place."

When she didn't move right off the bat, he offered her his arm as he had on their first date. "Shall we?"

"Okay." She took his offered arm. "But if you're trying to poison me so we can't look at apartments today, I'm tougher than I look. If I have to crawl into the apartments on my elbows, I will!"

"See? What'd I tell you? That's some cowgirl grit right there."

* * *

Vicky finished the last forkful of the best scrambled eggs she'd ever had. The grits were perfect, the biscuits with honey butter were amazing, and all the while, between her noises of pleasure from the tastiness of the food, Archer was sporting a very smug smile on his handsome face.

"Okay. I'll admit it."

"Admit what?" His chest puffed out.

"Well. Now, I'm not going to admit anything."

The waitress, Doris, came over to check on them. "You folks full? Or can I bring you a piece of pie? Homemade. Chocolate cream, lemon meringue, or apple."

Archer had told her that Doris, in her faded pink dress, teased bleached-blond hair, and red lipstick, was an institution at this restaurant and Vicky loved the fact that there was a history here. The diner had stood the test of time and had come out the victor.

"No. I'm stuffed," Vicky said. "The food was so good that I couldn't leave one bite."

Doris smiled at her as she started to take away some of the plates. "I'm glad you enjoyed it. What about some coffee?"

"Hot and black for me." Archer raised his eyebrow at Vicky and asked, "Decaf?"

Vicky nodded.

"Alrighty," Doris said. "One hot and black and one decaf. I'll be right back."

"And we'll take the check when you come back around next time."

More people were filing in and Doris greeted them right before she brought Archer and Vicky the coffees and the check. Vicky had been lying in wait for the check and when Doris put it down on the table, she snatched it up.

"Hey!" Archer complained. "It's my treat."

"No. It's my treat. You paid at Castillo's. I pay now."

"But you made lunch for me," he pointed out. "Four and a half grilled-cheese sandwiches."

"That doesn't count."

"It does."

"Well, if we can't agree, then it makes sense for us to pay our own way."

Archer took a sip of his coffee and then admitted defeat. They would split the check.

After their coffee, they paid their bill and headed out to his truck. All of her life, she had looked at these giant trucks with disdain. They took up too much of the road, they made her feel like a bug to be squashed in her sensible compact Subaru SUV, and they used up too much gas or diesel to be environmentally friendly. And yet, sitting up high, seeing the world from that vantage point, she kind of got it. Big trucks were fun.

"So where to?" Archer pushed the button to start the engine. "We've got some time to kill."

It took Vicky a moment to respond because her nose was too busy enjoying the woodsy, masculine scent of her companion. The man smelled sexy, and she couldn't stop her body from revving up like a rocket about to launch.

"Vicky?"

"Hmm." She came back down to earth. "Yes. Time to kill. There is a lovely park across from Bronco city hall. Up for a walk in the park?"

"Ten-four, cowgirl."

Whenever Archer called her a cowgirl, she was pretty surprised that it didn't irritate her. She was a Montana native—albeit a hippier version of a Montana girl. But, perhaps, just being around ranch and cowboy life had ingrained some cowgirl traits. Either way, she liked it.

Before they went to the park, they drove past a small bungalow that had a small backyard to match. This was one of the two places she would be seeing today. The second property was a third-floor walk-up in a refurbished brick building that had been, during its heyday in the 1900s, a hardware store.

"I think the bungalow would be my first choice," Vicky said thoughtfully. "I'd like my child to have a backyard to explore."

Archer nodded as he pulled into a parking spot near the park. "You could build a swing set. A sandbox. Make a garden so your child can have fresh vegetables."

Something in the way Archer was talking about the many uses for the backyard and speaking about her unborn child so lovingly, without some underlying motive or hidden agenda, caused her to almost tear up. It was touching and upsetting all rolled into one. Not that she wanted Louis back—she didn't. During one of the very few times they had discussed the pregnancy, Louis had denied the baby was his. Louis had demanded a paternity test and stated that the child would never be accepted by his parents. This was her baby and to discover that the biological father didn't want it had been, and still was, devastating.

Bringing her thoughts back to the present, she composed herself just in time as Archer opened the passenger door, helping her safely down to the ground. Even for May, there was a sweet scent in the air and a light breeze as they began to walk on the sidewalk that meandered through the old trees and their sprawling canopies. There was a fountain in the center of the park and they both seemed to head that way without discussing it.

"Wait!" Archer stopped, leaned down, and picked up a penny. "Head's up. That's good luck, Vicky."

He handed it to her and said, "Make a wish and throw it into the fountain."

Vicky took the penny, walked up to the fountain, closed her eyes, made a wish, and then tossed it into the water. The penny made the tiniest of splashes and Vicky silently hoped that it had the power to make her wish come true.

They strolled through the park, often in comfortable silence. She couldn't explain it and couldn't quite fathom it, but being with Archer was more comfortable than being around her own mother. Her own father. The comfort she felt with Archer was near the levels of Cassie and May Bell, and those relationships were years in the making. They were her closest and most trusted friends and confidantes.

"This looks like a good spot." Archer nodded to a bench pleasantly situated beneath one of the oldest oaks. In the limbs of that massive tree, there was life—bees buzzing around, birds chirping, and squirrels chasing each other up the trunk and across the heavy limbs before they leapt to the nearby branches of another oak tree.

The bench faced city hall and downtown Bronco. There was a nice feeling in Bronco—full of history and quaintness. Bronco was a larger town, bustling with more life than Tenacity. But it did have some similarities to Tenacity, which, she supposed, made her feel at home here.

"Thirsty?" Archer asked.

She nodded. "Maybe a ginger ale or a root beer?"

Archer got up, turned toward her and said, "Don't go anywhere."

That made her laugh. "I won't."

Archer walked away with that confident swagger and Vicky did appreciate his sexy rancher persona. But what she had already grown to love about Archer was his authenticity, his kindness, and his wonderful sense of humor. Many people in Tenacity had judged her character without knowing her. Perhaps she had done the same with Archer as she had once with Graham?

"Why now?" Vicky asked aloud. Why had the universe put Archer in her path at what she had determined was the absolute wrong time?

It hurt, like a tangible pain in her body, that her child was going to enter this world without a father. She wished that she could have given her baby a father like Archer. Solid. Willing. Loving. She had deeply loved her child the moment she'd found out she was pregnant, and that love for her child had helped her come to terms with the fact that, with Louis as her child's biological father, a part of her would love him as well. This had not, and would not, change her opinion of Louis's fitness to be a loving, caring father at this stage of his life. Why couldn't she give her baby the best kind of father? Didn't her child deserve that?

"Yes." She answered her own question. "My child does deserve that."

Archer crossed the main street of Bronco, back to his awaiting companion. There were so many land mines that he could step on and blow up his chances, however slim, with Vicky. Had the surprise of a baby thrown him? Sure. It would anybody, he reckoned. But he could no longer pretend that his feelings for her were strictly friendly. She was the whole deal—pretty, sweet, kind, thoughtful, and loyal. He wanted to get to know her better. He wanted to ask more questions. Yet, he didn't. Scaring Vicky off at this vulnerable, unstable time in her life could end things for good for them, even their fragile friendship.

"Here you go." He handed her a root beer.

She smiled at him. "Thank you."

"My pleasure." He joined her on the bench.

"Archer?"

"Yes."

"I'm sorry I've been all over the map. One minute I am going out to dinner with you, the next I'm telling you I can't see you because I can't get into a relationship, and then I accept your invitation to the dig, only to tell everyone we weren't really together. Then we leave the dig and I wind up asking you up for lunch."

"Those were epic grilled-cheese sandwiches."

"After cooking you lunch, I tell you I'm pregnant and can't see you anymore. Then—"

"You call me later to apologize, and you agree to let me drive you today."

She nodded with a pensive expression on her face. "Now, here we are."

"Hey. Look. I want to be here. I want to be there for you. Right now, you need a friend."

She nodded. "We are starting to be friends, aren't we?"

"I'd like to think so."

After she was silent for a couple of heartbeats, she asked, "Why doesn't it bother you? The way people think about me and my family?"

"I don't scare easy." Archer stretched out his legs. "Actually, I don't scare at all." So, deciding he perhaps shouldn't be afraid of a *few* land mines, he asked, "When are you thinking of moving?"

"Well." She put her hand on her rounded belly. "My community service is over in a month, and I'll be five months along in my pregnancy, so not so easy to hide."

"But why do you have to leave Tenacity? It's your home, just as much as anyone else's. Why do *you* need to move? If they don't like you, let them move!"

He knew he sounded riled, but it was his true self. Why should Vicky leave, possibly cutting short this thing between them before they even had a chance to figure out what it actually was?

"I really don't care what people think of me at this point. Some blame me for the entire economic downturn of our town."

He shook his head. "Idiots."

"And some just pity me because of my parents' sins," she said. "But I'm not leaving because of that. I'm leaving to give my baby a better life. How will my child be treated with all of the baggage I come with?"

Archer wanted to say, "If you were a Callahan, you'd have a family that would always have your back." But he didn't. Little by little, Vicky was opening up to him and he didn't want to do anything to make her close back up again.

Vicky's phone chimed and she said, "Time for my first appointment."

This inevitable chore had come too quickly. Would he be driving Vicky to her next home, a place she would move to in a matter of a month? Tenacity was his heritage and his home. He was a fourth-generation rancher—that was less about what he did on a daily basis and more about who he was at his core. He'd never leave Tenacity. He'd get married in Tenacity, raise his kids on the ranch, and grow old watching them make their own lives. All of it in Tenacity. If he couldn't find a way to get Vicky to stay in town, she would be lost to him forever.

"Okay, little darlin'." Archer stood and offered Vicky his hand. "Let's get 'er done."

Archer pulled up in front of the bungalow and Vicky just loved it. Yes, the front yard was unkempt and devoid of any cheerful color, but it had potential. A good spruce-up was all it needed.

The Realtor opened the front door to the house and waved.

"Victoria!" Susan Griffen said. "It's good to see you!"

Susan had graduated with Brent, and Vicky had decided that, while she wanted to keep her move under wraps, having a Realtor she knew might just help her avoid pitfalls in the rental market.

Vicky shook Susan's hand and then introduced Archer.

"Archer Callahan!" Susan smiled broadly at the rancher.

Vicky smiled briefly. Women of all ages reacted to Archer that way. He was the honey to every female bee in Montana. Whoever Archer married would just have to know that her husband was always going to draw female attention.

Susan tossed her hair a bit and tilted her head playfully when she said, “Now, Archer, I’m still waiting for you to call about that date you promised me.”

Then the Realtor laughed and held up her left hand, wiggling her fingers. “Just kidding! Happily married.”

She jiggled the house keys in her hand. “This isn’t about me. This is about the two of you.”

Vicky glanced up at Archer’s face to see if he was going to set Susan straight about the “two of you” comment. He hadn’t even so much as flinched.

Susan led them up to the bungalow. “So, as you can see, there is a lovely front porch here. You just need a couple of rocking chairs and you’ll be right at home. This house comes with a carport, so you’ll never have to park on the street.”

“That’s good,” Vicky said. “And that’s a playground across the street?”

“It surely is,” Susan said, opening the front door. “Perfect for a growing family.”

Vicky walked into the small living room that sported pea-green shag carpet to match the pea-green drapes. The living room was tiny, but she was used to tiny, and her furniture would fit.

“This home was built in 1935,” Susan explained. “Great bones. Just a little TLC is needed.”

“It smells musty in here,” Vicky noted with a wrinkled nose.

Susan nodded. “A bit like a wet dog. Yes. But the owner is willing to update the flooring if you sign an eighteen-month lease.”

They walked into the galley kitchen with mustard-yellow appliances. Vicky noticed that Archer had to duck to get into the front door, then to miss a chandelier in the living room, and again to enter the kitchen that was really too small for two much less three, particularly when the third was a six-foot-three rancher.

There was one bathroom, one bedroom, and a bonus room on their way to the backyard. Though earlier she'd been envisioning watching her child happily playing in the yard, when she stepped outside, her excitement plummeted. The yard was a pad of broken concrete overtaken by weeds pushing through the cracks. The chain-link fence was damaged and completely unsafe for a child. A discarded grill had been tipped on its side and a kiddy pool, cracked by the beating sun, had some green water pooled to one side.

"Now," Susan said, "I know it's a mess. The previous tenants had to be evicted, which as you know can take a long while and a lotta money. The owner is in the process of cleaning this up."

"Okay." That was all Vicky could manage. Archer hadn't said a word on the house tour, but she could imagine what he would say. Regardless, the bottom line was it was her choice for her baby.

They went back inside and, on the way to the front door, Vicky stopped off at the cozy room. "This could be the nursery."

Archer nodded. "Could be."

Susan's eyes widened. "Are you expecting? Why didn't I know you were expecting?"

Now she had gone and done it.

"W-well…" she stammered, trying find the right words.

Archer put his arm around her shoulders and said, "We are expecting. But we've been keeping it quiet for now."

Vicky didn't know if she wanted to elbow him hard in his ribs or kiss him for getting her out from a rock and a hard place.

While Susan did seem surprised that a Callahan would ever abandon Callahan Canyon, the Realtor just kept right on smiling. "Well, congratulations! With the playground and the backyard, once it's fixed up, this will be a perfect starter home."

"It is," Vicky said. "I'd like to review the lease agreement and if everything looks good, I'll sign and pay the deposit. You don't even have to show me the other apartment. This is the one."

She wasn't in love with the place, but the clock was running out for her. She needed to know where she would land and then start getting ready for the arrival of her baby. She could make this work.

Beaming, Susan clasped her hands and said, "Wonderful! It seems that opposites attract! Of course, I'm afraid you will have some bumps on your forehead, Archer. But that's a small price to pay."

Vicky met Archer's eyes as he said smoothly, "That's exactly right."

Chapter Six

"That was objectively horrible," Vicky said, perched up high in the passenger seat of Archer's truck.

"What was horrible?"

"Susan! Thinking that you were the father and possibly my husband? When I decided to use Susan, I didn't anticipate I'd have a Callahan as my plus-one."

"No. That went great. Don't worry. Things have a way of working out for us Callahan men."

"Okay. That may be true. I'm not a Callahan man. I'm Vicky Woodson and things always have a way of going wrong for me."

Vicky felt sick. Even though Susan was very active on all socials, Vicky had picked her because, historically, she was rather tight-lipped as a successful businesswoman who wanted to keep being successful. But Vicky showing up pregnant with Archer? Even a vault would have to spill those beans.

After several miles of silence, Archer said, "Look… There's been something I've been wanting to ask you, but it's never seemed like the right time."

She turned her head and body to look at him. "And now that I'm being held hostage in your tree house of a truck? That's the right time?"

"You love my truck, don't you?"

Vicky had to smile because, in her entire life, she'd never been impressed with cowboys driving around in jacked-up trucks, the bigger the tires, the closer to God type of deal.

Compensating for something, in her opinion. But now, since riding in Archer's truck, she had discovered a fondness for riding up so high.

"I'd heard a rumor that you aren't so fond of ranch life."

"It's not that simple," she said, not really wanting to go down the Stronk family ranch experience that seemed to be attempting to erase one hundred years of progress.

"Would you mind explaining it to me?"

"Um." She stalled a bit for time while she collected her thoughts. "I've always enjoyed being on Brent's ranch. I always felt happy there, helping with the chores, especially the chickens. I love them. But I have never seen myself there. There's a real part of me that longs for a more urban life. That's one of the reasons I like Bronco or even San Diego or Seattle."

"Those are a long way off."

"They are," she agreed. "But they seem to call to me."

He was quiet, so she added, "I was actually surprised that Cassie became a ranch-life convert."

Archer said, in a lower tone than he had been using, "Love can make people do amazing things."

She nodded in agreement, her hands resting on her rounded belly. What she didn't add was that sometimes love made people do amazingly bad things. Just look at her mother.

"I hate to admit this," Vicky added. "Especially as a native Montanan. But I'm scared to death of horses."

Archer looked over at her. "I can fix that."

She laughed with a shake of her head. "Are you ever unsure of yourself?"

Archer's eyebrows drew together, his face handsome from every angle and in every possible light.

"Rarely," he said, then followed that with a question. "Wanna make a wager?"

She shook her head. "No. I don't have time for a wager. Especially one that involves horses. Pretty to look at, but only at a very safe distance."

Archer shook his head and— Wait! Did he cluck at her? He had the unmitigated audacity to *cluck* at her! Those were fighting clucks. Now, she may not be a dyed-in-the-wool Montana cowgirl, but she was still a badass Montana woman who didn't back down from a fight.

"On second thought, I think I can work in a wager in between packing," she said. "What are the terms?"

"If I win and cure you of your fear of horses, I get to take you out on another date. A real date."

"And if I win," Vicky said confidently, "you help me move to Bronco."

Archer held out his hand for her to shake. "I hope you're not a sore loser," he said.

"I am," she retorted. "So, it's a good thing I don't lose. *Ever.*"

"Well, little cowgirl," Archer said with a cocky grin, "that streak is about to end."

He was carrying his toolbox up the narrow stairwell to Vicky's apartment when Archer realized that he had been outsmarted by his pretty auburn-haired companion. He had wanted to ask her a serious question; one he had been wanting to ask but could never find the right time. And she had craftily changed the topic to ranch life and horses, derailing his request.

Vicky opened the door and stepped aside for him to enter. Archer had to duck to avoid hitting his head on the way into the apartment where the ceiling inside didn't offer him much clearance either.

"Water?" she asked him from the kitchen.

"Sure."

He put down his toolbox and surveyed the damage he had done when he had made the questionable decision to sit in that flimsy egg chair.

"You really don't have to fix it." Vicky handed him a glass of ice water. "It was pretty much on its last leg when I found it at a swap meet."

"I've got to do it," Archer told her. "Raised up right."

Vicky sat down on the love seat. "Then I wouldn't dream of standing in the way of the Callahan family code."

He smiled at her, and he almost dropped his drill at the sight of her. Vicky was bathed in a ray of late-afternoon light that kissed her porcelain skin with gold and brought out the natural gold highlights in her long, thick locks. Those lips. Those eyes. He was mesmerized by her. The feeling he had for this woman, so quick and totally unexpected, sent him off-kilter.

"Everything okay?" Vicky asked.

He nodded, cleared his throat a couple of times, grabbed his glass that had been left an arm's length away on the tiny dining table, guzzled down the last of the water, and then focused his attention on the job at hand, not on the delectable Miss Woodson.

What would she do if I tried to kiss her?

"Sock me, most likely," he muttered under his breath.

"I'm sorry?"

He shook his head. "Nothing. Just working out the right way to fix this."

While he started to repair the chair, Vicky began to water her plants, talking and humming to each one.

"You've got a nice voice."

"Oh." Vicky sent him a bashful smile. "Thank you. Not really. The plants like it, though."

"I like it, too."

It didn't take him long to fix the chair. He pushed it back and forth, looking at the screws he had just put into place.

"Want to give it a whirl?" he asked.

"Absolutely." Vicky put down her sunflower watering can.

Finding gifts for Vicky wouldn't be difficult; just find something with a sunflower on it.

The mother-to-be sat down and she bobbed a bit before pushing off with her feet.

"Well?" he asked.

She looked up at him, beaming, "It's better than before."

"Good." He winked at her. "That's what I was aiming for."

Archer packed up his tools before he sat on the love seat with the flat cushions and broken springs. He could fix that, too. He could fix just about anything he put his mind to, actually. Maybe he could fix things in Vicky's life, not just her furniture.

"I'd like to ask you something." Archer stretched out his legs.

Vicky stopped swinging and her face turned ashen. She sensed what he wanted to ask was going to be a topic she wished to avoid. But he felt like he *needed* to know, not just wanted to know.

"What's Stronk's role in all of this?"

A dark cloud brushed over Vicky's face. Her eyebrows were drawn together and she frowned.

"His role? Almost nonexistent."

"What a snake in the grass." Archer felt both angry and protective of Vicky and her child.

"Look, I know how everyone in my life feels about Louis. I share many of them. But he is the father of my child. He may never have an active role, but that will never change who he is in my child's life. If later, down the road, he wants to have a relationship with our child, I will cross that bridge then. For now, he's in the background only."

"He's always been a dirtbag." Archer rested his forearms on his thighs. "How'd you get mixed up with him, anyhow?"

The minute those words passed his lips, Archer knew he had finally stepped on a land mine.

Vicky stood. "I'm tired. Thank you for the ride. I'm happy to reimburse you for the diesel and the food."

He stood up as well. “Vicky, I’m sorry. I mean it. I shouldn’t have said that. I’m just so damn mad that anyone would abandon the mother of their child! I’ve always wanted to have a family and here Stronk has everything I’ve wanted—a special woman like you, a child on the way.”

“Look.” Vicky seemed angry now and he was kicking himself for bringing up Stronk. “Other than Cassie, May Bell, Brent, and Sage, I didn’t have anyone. Louis acted like he didn’t care about the scandal. But then, bit by bit, little by little, he pulled away and then all he seemed to care about was the scandal. His parents didn’t approve of me. That’s the story and I’m actually growing weary of repeating it.”

“I’d still like to punch that arrogant smirk off his face.”

Vicky turned away from him to walk to the door. “I don’t need saving, Archer. Not by you, not by anyone. I don’t want Louis in my child’s life for now. After the paternity test confirms he’s the father, he will sign his parental rights away and I will sign an agreement freeing him from child support. A clean break and a fresh start for both of us.”

Archer picked up his toolbox, feeling like the lowest of the low. This was not how he had expected things to play out. And he couldn’t think of one way to get himself out of the mud puddle he was currently occupying. He could always talk his way out of something. Why couldn’t he do it with Vicky?

“I’m truly sorry, Vicky. I am.”

She nodded, her features drawn tight.

“Vicky,” Archer said. “Please, look at me.”

When she did look up at him, he did what he had only done once before, he opened the window to his soul and said, “I care for you, Vicky. I feel *connected* to you. I mean it sincerely.”

Arms crossed, Vicky said, “I know you do.”

Vicky’s shoulders dropped, as did her head. He caught the glassiness of her eyes as tears began to form, but she didn’t let them fall. Archer put his toolbox down and hugged her. She was stiff in his arms and then, for just a moment, she leaned on him and allowed him to hold her before she pulled away.

"Forgive me," Archer said. "I didn't mean to upset you."

She nodded. "I know you didn't. Louis is a…" She swallowed hard and continued, "A tough subject."

He gritted his teeth to bite back expletives with Louis Stronk's name on them.

"Where do we go from here?" he asked her.

"I don't know."

Archer knew that Vicky was different from other women he had known. She wasn't easily swayed by his charm, good looks, and the clout the Callahan name carried. Yet, what could he lose if he didn't at least try? Perhaps everything he truly wanted in his life.

"How about Tenacity Social Club?"

Vicky's face registered shock. So did her eyes. "Let me get this straight. After all of that, you're asking me out on a date?"

"Looks that way."

"You are insufferable."

"And hungry."

Vicky's expression changed from angry and annoyed to a look she might give a rambunctious puppy.

"Okay," she agreed. "But I'm picking up the tab."

Vicky walked into a packed Tenacity Social Club and immediately regretted accepting the invitation for an early dinner. It was Saturday and it felt like everyone in town was there.

"It looks slammed in here," Vicky said.

"We're already here," Archer said. "Besides, everywhere will be packed."

Archer found them two empty stools at the bar and the bartender greeted them. Michael Cooper, the bartender prided himself on knowing everyone's drink, so without asking, he delivered a bottle of beer to Archer and a lemon drop martini to her.

She shook her head and pushed the drink back. "Can I have a seltzer water with a lemon wedge instead, please?"

All of the activity of the day was making her feel slightly nauseous. On her nightstand, there were a ton of baby books she had read and reread. She hadn't had much morning sickness, and she felt lucky for it. That was one of the reasons she hadn't immediately thought *I'm pregnant* when her period was late. Besides, she had always been irregular. Lately, though, she had heartburn and her OBGYN attributed it to stress.

"Are you okay?" Archer leaned his head down to ask the question for her ears only.

She nodded, taking a sip of the bubbly seltzer.

Then she heard the loud, slurred voice of a woman who loved to stir up situations so she could sit back and watch the drama for her own entertainment.

"Vicky and Archer sitting in a tree, *k-i-s-s-i-n-g*. First comes love, then comes marriage and then comes Louis Stronk's baby in a baby carriage."

Archer stood, his neck red, his face angry. "Mind your own damn business."

The woman held up her bottle of beer and swung it around. "Hey. It's your wallet, Callahan. But me? I wouldn't want to foot the bill for a kid that's not mine."

Vicky was used to being in the spotlight, but how did this woman know she was pregnant? Couldn't it be that she simply hadn't wanted the lemon drop martini? More often than not, she didn't drink.

She handed her bank card to the bartender, at the same time trying to get Archer's attention. While that was happening, Cassie was blowing up her phone. Texting. Calling. Trying to video chat.

"And for your information," Archer said loudly, "this is my fiancée and this is my baby. Don't expect to be invited to the wedding!"

Suddenly her mind focused only on Archer. What had he just said?

She heard Cassie's worried voice coming through the phone, but she was frozen in her spot.

"Let's get out of here." Archer took out his wallet, slammed down a few bills on the bar and then put his arm around her shoulders.

Bank card in hand, Vicky said on the way out, "I already paid for your beer."

"Never mind." Archer brushed it off. "People really need to stick to their own business and keep their noses out of mine."

"Vic!" Cassie's urgent voice through the phone got her attention.

"Are you okay?" Vicky asked, still walking swiftly to keep up with Archer's long strides.

"Look at the *Tenacity Tattler*. Right now!"

Vicky had that same hollow feeling in her stomach when something horrible was going to break in the media. With the *Tattler* open, she saw a picture of Archer and her in front of the Off the Market sign with a caption: The Perfect Spot to Bring Baby Home. Welcome to Bronco, Archer and Vicky!

"Oh, no." Vicky stopped walking.

Archer had taken several long steps before he stopped, turned and came back to her.

"That's how she knew."

"Knew what?" Archer asked.

Vicky showed him the picture, then said to Cassie, "That's not the worst of it."

"What could be worse?" her best friend asked.

"Archer just told everyone at the social club that the baby is his and we are engaged."

Her whole world was coming apart at the seams while Archer sat at her kitchenette table inhaling a pizza they'd had delivered from Pete's Pizza.

"You're sure you don't want a piece?" he asked.

"No. I'm not hungry anymore."

"Well…" He polished off the last piece. "I think better on a full stomach."

Vicky felt numb. Completely numb. Why couldn't she stop making giant mistakes in her life? She'd accepted an invitation for dinner with Archer in order to give the town gossips some juicy red meat while she figured out her next moves with baby on board. Now, not only did everyone know she was pregnant, but Archer had also announced their engagement! Her ill-conceived plan had backfired. Majorly.

Sitting in the fixed egg chair, Vicky ignored the flurry of phone calls, the text messages, the notifications on the *Tenacity Tattler* page.

"What have you done, Archer?"

Archer sat down on the love seat. "I defended you and our baby."

Vicky felt confused. Blindsided. "This isn't *your* baby, Archer. And I'm not your fiancée."

She dropped her head into her hands. Everything she had done to repair her reputation in Tenacity was ruined. At the very least, people in town would think she was a jezebel trying to pin her baby on Archer. Even worse, they would think she was a two-timer who didn't know who the heck the father was.

"Well…" Archer leaned back, looking much more relaxed than he had a right to be. "Why not?"

Vicky lifted her head in disbelief. "Why not what?"

"Why can't we get married?" he asked. "Why can't I be a father for your baby?"

She could not process his words. All she could say was, "Are you crazy?"

"What? Why?" he asked in a tone that sounded the tiniest bit hurt.

A knock on the door stopped her from beginning to share the

very long list of reasons she felt he was plum crazy. She opened the door and was immediately embraced by Cassie.

Vicky let her in, shutting the door tightly behind her. She needed her best friend, now more than ever.

"Mint-chocolate-chip." Cassie held out the grocery bag.

"I'll get the spoons."

"Hey, Cassie."

Cassie walked over to Archer and punched him in the arm. "What did you do, Archer Callahan?"

"I didn't do anything," he said. "Other than take out your best friend."

"I said to take her out, show her a good time, not announce to the entire town that she's pregnant and you're engaged!"

"I was riffing," Archer said.

Cassie was midsentence when another knock on the door had her hang a U-turn. Graham was at the door.

"Hey, babe." Graham kissed Cassie. Then he turned to his brother. "What the heck did you do, Archer?"

Archer stood up. "Why does everyone keep pointing the finger at me?"

He went into the kitchen, pulled open a drawer, and then brought a spoon over to the table to join the women for some ice cream.

"Dude," Cassie said. "Boundaries. There's only enough for two."

"I'm still hungry." Archer frowned at them. "I only had a pizza."

"Yes," Vicky said. "An entire large pizza!"

"Callahan men," Cassie explained to her. "It's hard to keep food in the house."

Graham milled around, looking awkward, and then he hit his head on the fan above the small coffee table. "There isn't enough room for four people in this shoebox." Graham pulled the egg chair, with its frame, over to the table so he could join them. He squeezed his body into it but looked completely uncomfortable. "Bro," Graham said, "what did we just talk about?"

Cassie frowned at him. "What does that mean?"

Now Graham looked even more uncomfortable. "Just that it wasn't a good idea to date a woman who was pregnant. I don't think that, at this point, he is ready to be a father. That's all. I didn't mean anything bad by it, Vicky."

"You didn't mean anything *bad* by it?" Cassie asked.

"No. I didn't," Graham said but he sounded like he was trying to backpedal, and Vicky had never seen Archer's older brother so flustered. "Just giving my little brother some advice. And sorry, brother, but you do have a history of riding to the rescue on a proverbial white horse. Nothing wrong with that."

"Well, your advice stinks," Cassie said. "Vicky is my best friend, and any man would be lucky to have her as his wife."

"Point taken." Graham used a conciliatory tone. Then he asked, "Could I get some of that mint-chocolate-chip?"

"This isn't going anywhere good for you," Archer said to his brother.

"Yeah." Graham sighed. "I know."

Cassie blew out a breath, stood, and stomped into the kitchen to retrieve a spoon for her fiancé. She handed it to him and said, "This isn't the last of it."

"Yeah." Graham dug his spoon into the ice cream. "I know."

The four of them made short work of the gallon of ice cream and then Archer said, "I admit I went off half-cocked."

Vicky, her best friend, and his brother all looked at him wordlessly.

"But let me ask you this," he continued. "Is it really a crazy idea?"

Graham spoke first. "Damn right, it's a crazy idea."

"Why?" Archer sat straighter in his chair, like he was brewing for a fight. "Look at the two of you. You needed a wholesome girl-next-door that everyone in the town loved to make you a more attractive candidate for voters in the mayoral race."

Then Archer pointed at Cassie. "And you wanted a date to your sister's wedding! And now the two of you are a couple."

Vicky had to admit that what Archer had said was true. But lightning just didn't strike twice.

The look in Archer's green eyes was so sincere when he said, "You don't want to leave Tenacity, Vicky. You don't."

She nodded. "No. I don't. But I can't stay here and allow my child to be treated badly because of the sins of the mother and the grandparents."

"You and your child would have the protection of the Callahan name," Archer said to her. Then, to Cassie and Graham, he challenged, "Neither one of you can deny that."

They couldn't, so they didn't. Even though Cassie and Graham were in the small space with them, somehow, they seemed to fall away, and it was only Archer and Vicky.

"Why would you do this for me, Archer?" Vicky asked. "What's in it for you?"

Archer held her gaze, so she could see the honesty in his eyes. "I need to lay my cards out on the table here. I've always had feelings for you, Vicky. I do. And there might be something between us. I feel it and you feel it."

She gave the tiniest of nods in agreement.

"If you marry me, you could stay right here in Tenacity where you belong." He made his case. "And you and me, we'll have some time to figure out if this thing between us, that we both feel, is more than just friendship. Now, who in this room can tell me what's so damn wrong with that?"

Chapter Seven

Archer sat at Vicky's table, hemmed in between Graham and Cassie, wondering to himself what the heck he had gone and done. But he was in it now. He'd been a goof-off most of his life. Whatever way the wind blew, that was his life strategy. This was different and the only way he knew to navigate it was just to move forward and figure it out as he went.

Archer stood up. "Now, what I need to do is to ask you guys to leave."

"Me?" Cassie pointed at herself.

"Yes," Archer said. Vicky was watching him with what he read as shock on top of shock.

"You're asking me to leave?" his brother asked, incredulous.

"Yes."

"Vic?" Cassie checked with her friend.

Vicky breathed in deeply and let it out slowly, her eyes tired. "I think it's for the best, Cass. We've got to work our way through this."

Cassie and Graham rose, hugged them both, and then headed out. But not before Cassie said loud enough for him to hear, "If you need me for anything, Vicky, I am a mere text away."

"I love you," Vicky said before she closed the door.

Archer stood with his hands in his pockets, watching Vicky with a keen eye. The mother-to-be, shoulders down, rested her forehead on the door before turning back to him.

"I'm tired," Vicky told him.

"I know you are."

"This is a mess."

"I know that, too."

Vicky slumped down onto the couch, kicked off her sandals, and leaned back, hugging one of the deflated pillows. She closed her eyes, and Archer had the same inclination to protect the pretty Miss Woodson that he'd had since their first date. He'd told her he followed his gut, and that's what he'd continue to do.

"This isn't how I thought the day would end." Archer sat down at the table, let his long legs stretch out to the side.

Vicky's eyes cracked open. "Nope. Didn't call it."

In a short span of time, both their phones were chiming, and ringing, and notifying, and being annoying as all get-out. Archer turned off the volume on his phone while Vicky bravely reviewed her messages.

She sat forward, head in her hands. "Oh, my Lord. My mom, my dad, my brother, May Bell. I have been tiptoeing around this town trying to lay low and now I've managed to throw the Woodson name right back into the fire.

"Of course, Susan posted the picture on the *Tenacity Tattler*. Of course she would," Vicky grumbled. "The only people who knew I was pregnant were Louis, Cassie, and you."

"And Graham."

"Because you told him."

"Yep." Archer ran his fingernails over the stubble on his face.

"Now, everyone knows! Everyone!" Vicky let out her frustration. "And that I'm moving to Bronco. All my personal information on blast!"

Archer rubbed his hand over his face. "Well, you had some help with that."

Vicky nodded, stood, and sat down heavily at the table. "Yeah. What gives, Archer?"

"I don't know." He owed her honesty. "I said what came to mind."

She rested her chin in her hand, her eyes staring off. "What should I do now?"

He reached for her free hand. "Marry me, Vicky. What do you have to lose?"

Vicky didn't pull her hand away and that was, at least, a positive sign.

"You're serious about this?"

"I am." He looked her square in the eye. "Let's do it. Let's get married. You want to be here to support your family. Even though they did wrong, they're still your parents."

Vicky nodded.

"You don't have to travel to Bronco any more to see a doctor. You can see one right here. A new practice just opened. Why give birth alone in Bronco? Cassie's here. Brent's here. May Bell is here."

He stopped and then felt emboldened to add, "I'm here."

Vicky seemed to drift for a minute or two before she looked back at him and said, "I may live to regret this, but yes, Archer. I will marry you."

Damn, but he felt like smiling for the first time since the scene at the social club.

Archer took Vicky's hand that he had been holding, kissed it, and then said with a half smile, "You never know, Miss Woodson. You may just live to love it."

The next day, with her secret out, Vicky felt like the weight of the world had been lifted off her shoulders. Now, she didn't have to move and start a new life as a single mother. Yes, she knew people, like Susan, in Bronco because of their Tenacity connection, but they couldn't take the place of Cassie, Brent, May Bell, Sage, and, even, her parents. Having her first child was a dream come true. She wanted to share that joy with the people she cared about the most.

“May Bell.” Vicky entered the shop and walked directly into May Bell’s welcoming arms.

“Hey, sweetie.”

May Bell gave the best hugs. They were long and steady, and Vicky could feel total acceptance in that hug.

“I am so sorry.” Vicky felt near tears. “I just didn’t know how to tell you about the baby and the move. I promise that I had already started to make a list of some excellent prospects to help with the store and I could still scout for fresh merchandise.”

May Bell brushed off her worry. “You’ve done just fine, V. W. Bug. It’s true I have a tricky hip that acts real funny every now and again and the arthritis, the bursitis, and any other *-itis* a person can be afflicted with. But Emil always said, God rest his wonderful soul, that there wasn’t nobody tougher than May Bell Carter. I dearly miss that man, I surely do. But he was my one true love. I was lucky to have him. If you can find a love like that, dear, hold it in your hands so tightly that it hurts, and never let it go. That’s the best advice this old lady can give.”

“Thank you, May Bell. For understanding.”

“You get as old as me, you start to understand a whole lot more. The only problem then is remembering what you understood,” the shop owner said with a self-effacing smile and a wave of her hand.

Vicky was already aware that the fresh Woodson gossip had circulated quickly through Tenacity. Of course, May Bell’s quilting circle was one of the biggest stops on the gossip line.

The reaction to her lightning-speed betrothal to Archer, with baby on board, had mainly been met with confusion and shock. She had spoken with her parents while Archer had handled his other brothers, and she was to meet Brent for lunch later at the Silver Spur Café.

“Which brings us to Archer Callahan,” May Bell said.

“Yes,” Vicky said as she opened a new box of vintage clothes and began to hang them up on hangers. “Archer Callahan.”

Vicky filled May Bell in on the events that had transpired in a very short amount of time. It had been a whirlwind when she'd experienced it firsthand; she could only imagine how disorienting it was for her friends and family.

"And then he stood up and announced to the entire crowd at the social club that we were getting married and that the child I'm carrying was his."

"My word. What a scene."

"I know." Vicky began to put price tags on the just-arrived items. "I felt like one of those cartoon creatures that gets run over by a car and then stands back up completely flattened. I just couldn't believe that those words would ever come out of Archer's mouth."

May Bell took the tagged clothes to integrate them into the racks. "I don't think it's that out of character for him."

"You don't?"

"No," the elder woman said. "Archer has always been a romantic. He wants to be married, settle down and have a bunch of little Callahan children running about."

Vicky heard that description of Archer and the thought of this fake marriage turning into the real deal made her dizzy and lightheaded. She sat down in the nearby chair.

"What is it?" May Bell was by her side. "Is it the baby?"

Vicky breathed in a calming breath, then let it out. "It's everything, I think."

"Well, of course. You have been through the wringer, poor thing."

Vicky rested her hand over her growing belly. This was the first day since she'd found out that she was pregnant that she didn't feel the need to hide it. What a relief. She didn't have to try to hold in her tummy or wear increasingly baggy clothing. This was her baby belly, and she was proud to have it.

"I can't understand how this has all unfolded from one quick date at Castillo's." Vicky took the offered cold ginger ale from May Bell.

"I have heard that there is something special in their homemade salsa."

That brought a smile to Vicky's face. "But I'm so grateful. I don't want to overthink it if I can help it, trying to predict the future and how this all ends."

"No sense in that at all."

"I get to see a Tenacity OBGYN. I get to give birth right here, with my friends and family by my side."

Vicky paused, sensing some strong feelings trying to break through, but she stopped them and then continued, "And because of all of this, I believe I will always have love in my heart for Archer for this incredible gift he wants to give me and my child."

Vicky left Nothin' New after promising May Bell she would be back to close the store. Now she was on her way to meet Brent for lunch at the café on Central Avenue. She felt nervous to face Brent. Her love for her brother and his happiness had, like a domino effect, set off her confession about hiding the stolen money, and her mother's confession, and then her father's involvement and fall from grace. The only positive was the fact that Brent was able to repair his relationship with Sage. And, to scc her brother happy with his true love, Vicky knew she would do the same thing if she could go back in time. Yet, she'd just thrown the family back into the negative limelight, and Brent, for sure, wasn't going to be happy about that.

"Hey, Tori." Brent had found a table for them.

"Hey, Brent." She hugged him tightly.

They ordered and then it was time to face the music with her brother. As expected, his facial expression read concerned, frustrated, and incredulous.

"A baby?" Brent asked under his breath. "Why didn't I know about this, Tori?"

Vicky felt like she was a teenager being scolded by her dad.

"You were moving to Bronco, and you didn't tell me?" Now she could see deep hurt in Brent's eyes and, for that, she hurt as well.

"Once I found a place where I could land, I was going to tell you," she explained. "But then—"

"All heck broke loose."

She nodded. "I'm sorry. I didn't want to tell you right off the bat because I didn't want my secret to become your secret. A secret you would have to keep from Sage."

For a moment, Brent just sat there digesting those words. She knew he finally accepted her reasons when he reached for her hand, held it and squeezed it reassuringly.

Brent let out a frustrated sigh and looked around for close-by listeners before he asked, "Why marry Callahan? Marriage isn't something to enter into lightly, Tori. I'm engaged to Sage now and it's serious business."

Vicky frowned at him. "Don't you think I know that?"

"I don't know what you know, sis. What I do know is that you are marrying a man I have only seen you with once."

The waitress delivered their food, and Vicky took that opportunity to redirect the conversation. This was a skill she had learned as a teenager to keep her parents from bickering non-stop.

"Any news on the dig?" she asked Brent.

Brent wiped his mouth and then said, "Lynda Slater, Gideon Frost, and nearly every other lawyer in this town is working overtime to figure out Brad Bruckner's claim on the land. There's no way that this thing can be real. No way! But they've definitely halted the dig. The thing I want to know is why now? Dinosaur bones in Tenacity aren't news. There has to be something else that Bruckner wants. But what? What do they want?"

"I don't know but I believe our town will figure it out," Vicky said, finishing off her eggs. "There has to be more to the story, and I would bet the farm on Lynda and Gideon any day of the week and twice on Sunday."

Brent paid for the meal, and she left the tip. Together they walked outside to what was shaping up to be a beautiful Montana spring afternoon.

"Look, Tori, I'm worried about you," her brother said. "You've already been through so much. Are you really thinking through this marriage with Archer?"

"I know that this decision looks like I'm making yet another huge mistake in the long line of mistakes."

Brent nodded as she continued.

"But I am convinced that this is the right step for me and my baby."

"Why? Marriage isn't a magical cure for what ails you."

"I'll be able to have my baby here, surrounded by my friends and family. I've seen how the Callahan family has embraced Cassie after her girlfriend/boyfriend of convenience deal with Graham turned into real love. The Callahans are as close as family can be. They'll protect my baby from anyone in town who would want to take my mistakes, and our parents' mistakes, out on them. I'm not being impulsive, Brent. I'm being strategic."

She could tell that she was at least scoring some points with her brother. After some thought, Brent said, "I know you don't want to tell me who the father of this baby is, Vicky, but let's face it, you were dating Stronk two months ago. You look like you're farther along than that."

She couldn't disagree, so she didn't try.

"So, I can fill in the details myself," Brent continued. "What's in it for Callahan? What in the world is he doing and why is he inserting himself into our family drama?"

"The truth?"

"Of course."

"I'm not totally sure," she admitted. "But believe it or not, we have become friends. We just clicked. We just gelled."

"Like Sage and me."

"Yes. Just like that," she said. "Archer cares about me and I care about him."

The surprise on Brent's face made her smile. Brent wasn't often surprised.

"Well, then," he said somewhat begrudgingly, "I suppose I'll need to give him a chance."

She hugged her brother. "Thank you, Brent. I love you."

"I love you. Just be careful, Tori. Pay attention to the caution lights, okay?"

"I promise."

"Now," her brother asked, "when and where is this wedding going to take place?"

Archer was beat. He'd spent the day mainly fielding questions from his family about his sudden engagement to Vicky Woodson, along with answering texts en masse to his friends. When he'd declared his intention to marry Vicky, he was basically riffing. It wasn't something he had thought through until way after the fact. Even when he was busy convincing Vicky and Cassie and Graham that it was a great idea, he had been running on adrenaline. It wasn't until the next morning that he'd begun to feel the enormity of what he had set into motion. Now, after defending his decision to friends and family, all of their valid concerns had seeped into his brain and shifted his own thoughts.

"You did it again, didn't you, Arch?" he asked himself, driving off his family's ranch. Graham and Cassie had paved the way for his relationship with Vicky; and because his family had already gone through one recent fake-relationship-turned-real-deal, their reaction wasn't as explosive, but still fraught with concerns.

It was true that, in his early twenties he had made the mistake of trying to save women, to be their knight in shining armor, and it had cost him dearly. Perhaps no one would believe him, but he was sure that Vicky was different. His feelings for her were different. He didn't fully understand those feelings, but now, having Vicky in his life, perhaps he could sort those feelings out.

He parked his truck down the street from Nothin' New. He wanted to touch base with Vicky to figure out their next steps. Would she see on his face and in his eyes that doubts had crept in? He certainly hoped not.

Archer opened the door to the secondhand store only to be greeted by May Bell who ordered him to close his eyes.

Archer stopped and did as he was told. He heard May Bell spiriting away his fiancée to the back of the shop.

"Now you can open them," May Bell told him. "It's bad luck to see your bride in her dress before the wedding day. When is the wedding, by the way?"

"I think we still need to hammer those details out."

"Well—" May Bell eyed him with a direct gaze "—Vicky is platinum. You get my drift?"

"Yes, I do."

"Good," she said, pleased. "Then come over here and give me some sugar."

He was in the midst of a hug when he saw Vicky come out from the back of the shop, her thick, unruly auburn hair framing the delicate features of her face. His gut twisted, his knees felt rubbery and any second thoughts of marrying Vicky Woodson vanished like vapor.

"Sorry about that." Vicky was blushing and her skin had a glow. "I think I found my wedding dress."

"Correction." May Bell waved her hand. "You *have* found it."

Vicky hugged May Bell. “Thank you for the most wonderful gift.”

“My pleasure,” the elder said. “I have had this tucked away in the back room, just waiting to find the right woman. And now I have.”

May Bell left soon after, never wanting to be late for the quilting circle. Alone together for the moment, Archer gravitated toward his bride-to-be and she to him. They hugged, taking a moment of solace in each other’s arms. When he was with Vicky, he knew this marriage of convenience was the right move for him. She was special and he needed the time to figure out why.

“Would you like to take a stroll with me after you close up?” Archer asked her.

She nodded, tucking a loose strand of hair behind her ear. “That would be nice.”

“I’ll pick you up at five, then?”

He was leaving as a couple of customers came into the shop. Archer pushed on the door, paused, turned back to catch Vicky’s attention and he tipped his hat up in a show of cowboy respect. And, darn if it didn’t make her smile and blush a deeper shade of pink.

“Damn pretty,” Archer said of his fiancée. “Damn pretty.”

Vicky felt like she was floating on air for the rest of her shift. There was something in the way Archer had looked at her when he’d asked to take her on a stroll. It felt as if he was seeing her completely for the first time and he’d liked what he’d seen. She looked at the clock; five minutes until closing.

“Here you go.” She handed the bag to the customer, a woman she had spoken to a couple of times while working off her community hours at the Tenacity Dinosaur Center and Park. “The receipt is in the bag. Come see us again.”

“Oh, I will,” the customer said. “And by the by… I understand congratulations are in order. A baby and a Callahan? You've been busy."

"Thank you." Vicky followed the customer to the door, let her out and then locked it.

She quickly went through her nightly closing routine, justifying the register, putting the drawer money in the safe. She took one last look at the surprise dress May Bell had gifted to her, and then she set the alarm, turned off all the lights, and then locked the door behind her.

"Hi, there." Archer was leaning against the brick wall, one leg bent, cowboy hat casting his face in shadow.

"Hi, there, yourself."

Wasn't it funny that the mere sound of Archer's sultry baritone voice could send a rather naughty chill right down her spine? This wasn't the first time the handsome rancher had highjacked her mind and taken her to more *adult* scenarios.

"May I escort you, Miss Woodson?" Archer asked, holding out his elbow.

She looped her arm with his and they began to stroll, as if they didn't have a care in the world.

"Lots of stares coming our way," Vicky said in a low voice. "Everything going to plan?"

"So far, so good." He laughed. "May as well give folks what they want."

While they walked, Archer filled her in about his day telling his family about their plans. Not smooth going, but that was to be expected. She told him that she'd had a similar experience with her brother.

"But, in the end, they were supportive," Archer said. "They wanted to know if you've thought about what kind of wedding you want to have."

"Quick." That word popped out.

"A woman after my own heart."

She squeezed his arm and tilted her head toward his. Yes, it was good fodder to town gossips, but it had been brought on by true emotion. It was true what she'd said to Brent before. Archer and she just clicked. For now, just as friends and soon-to-be husband and wife. But who knew what the future held? Maybe this could turn into a true romance like Cassie and Graham's.

"I was thinking about having the wedding at Castillo's," she told him.

He thought about it and then nodded. "Our first date."

"Yes," she said. "It's also a one and done. Marriage vows and reception all at one venue."

"That's the ticket."

"Then I'll call Castillo's tomorrow and make a reservation? Do we have a date in mind?"

"The weekend after next."

Vicky felt like her head was spinning while at the same time her baby was practicing hip-hop moves in her belly.

"Everything okay?" he asked.

"I think I just felt my first kick. Baby on board must like the sound of your idea."

"Could I?" he asked sincerely.

"No. Not yet. But eventually," she said, still in wonder. "Life is a miracle,"

"It is."

Vicky turned to face him completely, took both of his hands in hers. "We are getting married."

Archer took her hand and kissed it. "Yes, Miss Woodson. We are definitely getting hitched."

Chapter Eight

Plans were underway for the thrown-together wedding at Castillo's. Vicky sent out e-vites to all of the guests—just a handful of their closest friends and family. Archer, who was turning out to be a romantic man beneath that tough rancher exterior, had suggested putting sunflowers at every table. Then she'd suggested they also put horseshoes in with the flowers, so they were both represented. Cassie, ever the best friend and fantastic party organizer, was indispensable to making a quick wedding happen.

"For a one-week turnaround, we are in great shape," Cassie said.

Holding the phone with one hand and opening the door to her apartment to let Archer in with the other, Vicky said, "I can't thank you enough, Cass."

"Isn't that what a best friend is for?"

"Well, you are the *bestest* of best friends." Vicky laughed. "I don't think that's a real word."

They exchanged promises to talk later before they hung up and Vicky was able to hug Archer. Over the last week, and as the wedding approached, they had grown close enough to hug each other and hold hands. It was beginning to feel more like a sweet courtship rather than a marriage of convenience.

"How are you?" she asked.

"I'm good."

He gulped down the water, put down the glass, and then said, "We've still got some things to iron out."

"Like a prenup?"

He shook his head. "No. If I didn't trust you, I wouldn't marry you, even if we were more than friends right now."

She waved her arm around the room dramatically. "Well, fair is fair, when we do get divorced, you can have half of all of this."

An emotion passed over his face but then it was gone so fast that she wondered if she had seen it all. Especially when he said with a smile, "The egg chair."

That made them laugh together. It felt good to laugh with Archer.

"It's yours." She smiled at him.

"That brings me to one of those things we need to iron out."

She waited for his next words.

"Where are we going to live?"

It was so silly, but in the haste of pulling the wedding off, she hadn't given much thought to what happened after she became Mrs. Archer Callahan.

"My place won't work," she noted.

"No," he agreed. "You can move into my cabin on the ranch."

She gave him a playful side-eye. "You are just determined to get me to like ranch life."

He winked at her. "You *are* marrying a rancher."

"Okay, then. Your place. I'll bring the egg chair."

Callahan Canyon Ranch made the most sense and, most likely, it wouldn't be a permanent deal. When a marriage of convenience became inconvenient for either of them, she would move on. Maybe even to a metropolitan city where she could live in a high-rise apartment and take her child to the beach and museums. "What's next on your groom's list?"

"I don't like wearing a suit coat," Archer told her. "Actually, I don't like wearing any part of a suit."

"What do you want to wear?"

"Clean jeans, boots, belt, button-down, hat, and the bolo tie May Bell gave me."

"Perfect."

"Okay." He looked taken aback. "You're sure?"

"Of course I am. I want you to be comfortable. Just because this wedding was born out of true friendship versus true love, why can't we enjoy it just the same?"

He studied her and she felt that same blush rise to her cheeks whenever Archer looked at her like he was now. He might not love her, but he was attracted to her, just as she was attracted to him. Yet she couldn't unlock the padlock on the part of her heart that fell in love. She had her baby to think about and going through another unexpected breakup, like with Louis, would throw her inner world into sadness and grief. No. She had to keep her mind straight, keep her romantic heart guarded from Archer, and always think first about her baby.

"We've got to get our marriage license at Tenacity Town Hall tomorrow or there isn't going to be a wedding this Sunday."

"I know. You're right. I'll let May Bell know that I'll be a tad late."

After they agreed on a time to get their license, which would then be followed with her visit to his cabin at his family's ranch the next day, Archer left to get back to his work on the ranch and she got herself ready for the last day of community service at the Dinosaur Center. Yes, her time there had been meaningful to her, and she had come to view her coworkers as friends. All of them had been already cordially invited to her wedding.

She got dressed and looked in her full-length mirror at her reflection, hands smoothing the material over her belly.

"I am so grateful for you," she said to her baby. "I can't wait to meet you."

And she just couldn't wait. The week after the wedding, she would have her first appointment with a local OBGYN. All of her records from Bronco had already been transferred to

Tenacity. She had, of course, let Susan know that she wouldn't be moving to Bronco, after all. Things seemed to be going so smoothly that part of her wondered when that next horrible shoe would drop. It seemed like it happened to her each and every time she was about to put her guard down and take a deep sigh of relief. She'd be sucked into a cyclone of bad news and scandal.

"That's okay," she told her baby as she opened the door to leave. "We've got this. We have Archer now and I won't think about the time when we won't have him. I'm just going to think about right now, today. We have Archer today. We have to be grateful for that."

Archer was feeling good about this decision. He was about to be a married man with a wife and a child on the way, and it had all, literally, transpired over two weeks. It was Friday and the wedding was on Sunday.

"Hi!" Vicky met him at the top of the stairs of Tenacity town hall.

"Hi, yourself." Archer held out his hand to help her with those last steps. Her baby belly was on full display in snuggly fit jeans and a ruffled, scoop-necked blouse. It seemed as if her belly had doubled in size overnight. Or perhaps his bride-to-be was more comfortable having that belly visible. Either way, it made him both excited for the baby to arrive and panicked enough to run in the opposite direction.

"Ready?" he asked her.

"Are you?"

He nodded. "We've come too far to back down now."

They stood in the short line, and Archer was more keenly aware of the stares they always drew when they were together. It was like they had become mini-celebrities, not always portrayed in the best light, but always noticed. It was annoying to him, actually. He now knew, firsthand, why Vicky had felt the need to start fresh with her child. Just in the last two weeks, Archer had become fed up and ready to start confronting people who couldn't mind their own business. Vicky was, to her credit, poised and stoic. As the daughter of two scandalized parents, one of whom had been the town mayor, his fiancée was well acquainted with the unflattering spotlight and being the main topic on the *Tenacity Tattler.*

"Next, please!" A worker waved them over.

"We'd like to get a marriage license," Archer said and he looked down at the pleased, shy smile of his bride-to-be. He reveled in the way Vicky looked right at that moment—face glowing, eyes dancing with happiness. Gone was the sad look in her eyes he had seen in the many online posts and in the town newspaper. And he felt good about himself because he had been the one to take that burden off her shoulders and take on that mantel. He had broad shoulders, and they could handle just about anything. In his mind, even when his feet were frozen in a block of ice, that was the impetus he needed to keep moving forward.

The clerk handed him a sheet of paper. "Fill out this form and turn it back in to me."

They took the form to a nearby table and began to fill in the boxes asking for date of birth, parents' names, address, and name of officiant. They had decided, in light of the fact that they both knew this was a marriage that would eventually dissolve, to not be married by a pastor or a priest. Instead, they settled on a justice of the peace in Tenacity.

"Education?" Archer asked her after filling out her parents' place of birth.

"Two years community," she said. "I don't even know that about you."

"Thirty years in ranching," he said with a wink.

Vicky pointed to the box asking Number of This Marriage and said, "This is my first. I don't have any past husbands lurking in the shadows. Don't worry. How about you?"

"I've got nothing to report," he said.

They finished the form, returned it to the window once the line moved, and handed it over with the small fee. Following a short wait, and after they'd signed the application, a marriage license was given to them.

"After the ceremony, the license must be returned to the clerk's office within thirty days for recording," the man said. "And congratulations. Next!"

On the way to Archer's family's ranch, Vicky held the marriage license. She had, of course, taken pictures and sent them to Cassie and her family. She had been very quiet on her socials ever since the scandal erupted when she'd come clean about her role in the stolen money. Part of her really wanted to post this document, primarily to show her followers, many of whom had been catty rather than consoling, that she had rebounded. She was marrying a super-handsome cowboy, and she had a baby on the way. But then she reminded herself that this marriage was temporary, not one meant to last.

"Are you ready?" Archer asked her.

They had pulled off the main road onto a gravel road with some potholes along the way. It was gorgeous ranch land as far as the eye could see. An iconic representation of ranch life in Montana: cows grazing, mountain peaks off in the distance, crystal-clear babbling brooks.

"Ready," she said, but she didn't feel so ready on the inside.

Archer took a left onto a less-defined road surrounded by trees with large, overreaching canopies. Then the canopies opened to a large clearing of land, revealing a rustic cabin, with a roughhewn porch and a tin roof, happily situated by a pond.

"First impression?" he asked.

"It's amazing, Archer." She surprised herself by saying, "I actually love it."

"Good." He made to get out of the truck.

"Wait." She stopped him. "I need to tell you something."

"Okay. I'm listening."

"I feel terrible about this, I really do. When I said yes to you for our first date, I was hoping that if I was seen with you, attention would be focused on that, making it easier for me to figure out next steps and keep my pregnancy a secret."

Archer looked at her without a word. Though she was unable to read his expression, she felt uncomfortable under his gaze.

Then he finally said, "You did what you had to do. Don't worry so much."

"Okay." She smiled self-consciously. "I'll try."

Together, they walked to the front porch and then Archer opened the door for her. She stepped into a rather stark interior—no rugs or window coverings, and a lone couch in the living area.

"I know." Archer shut the door. "It doesn't look like much right now. But not bad considering that I just moved in recently."

"It's fine." And she meant it.

"Let me give you the tour. Three bedrooms."

Vicky was smiling as Archer did his best to sell his cabin to her. It was these moments when she saw the kind man behind the macho exterior, and it made her like him even more.

"Whatever you want to do with the kitchen, the living room, bathrooms, anything, you have my full support."

"I can't do that," she said.

"Why not?"

"Because this is your permanent home. For me, it's…um… *not*."

Her fiancé seemed to dismiss that concern as he showed her the main bedroom. "This will be your room."

"No. I'm not going to kick you out of your own bedroom, Archer."

Still pushing on, seemingly oblivious to her comments, he showed her a small, cozy room that could be used as a nursery.

"I've just been storing things in this room. I'll clear it out. No big deal."

Vicky couldn't process all of the information coming at her at once. She could not, in good conscience, take over Archer's house. That had never been her plan.

"Why can't I stay in this room with the baby?" she asked.

"Nah." He shook his head. "I like my idea better. I can paint the walls any color you'd like. I think a crib would fit that wall nicely. It's a nice view but under a shade tree so it won't get too hot."

Vicky followed him back to the kitchen; he had managed to make a living plan for her and her baby without her input at all. She sat down on a wobbly counter stool, her brain shuffling through her shifting thoughts. She was very aware that this cabin was his, not hers. But at the same time, she did want to have some say in her life when she moved to the ranch.

Archer put a glass of water in front of her while he guzzled down one glass and then went in for a refill.

"You're unhappy," he said.

"No. Not *unhappy* exactly."

"You have that wrinkle between your eyes. That's your unhappy face."

How did he know so much about her in such a short time?

"Okay," she admitted. "I want to feel like I have a say in this, knowing, of course, that this is your home, not mine."

"Look, Vicky." Archer put his glass in the sink, leaned back against the counter, arms crossed in front of his body in a relaxed manner that showed off his large biceps without him trying one bit. "I know this is my home. But after Sunday, this is your home, too. We have to live *now*, not later. If you want to paint the nursery pink with green polka dots, have at it."

Vicky listened to him, but her frown was still in place.

"The reason I want you to take the main bedroom is because

you can access a bathroom without having to put on a robe just to get across the hallway."

Now she felt like she had overreacted.

"I guess that makes sense."

He laughed. "Don't worry, I don't expect an apology."

"Thank you for looking out for me and my baby."

"I am going to be your husband. That's my job."

After giving his bride-to-be the tour, Archer met his three brothers. They were moving a large herd of cattle. Two bulls from different herds managed to break through the electric fence and beat the heck out of each other. It was a tough job to get everything sorted out and Archer was already late.

"Good of you to show up!" Ash ribbed him.

"He's been slacking off, if you ask me," Cooper added.

Less good-naturedly, Graham said, "Stop bumping your gums and focus on this deal right here. Too damn dangerous to mess around!"

It wasn't often, but now and again, Graham would assert his position as the eldest of the four. And when he did, they all fell in line behind him. This was dangerous work and they had to be laser focused on getting the herds back in order. The bulls had always been cut out of the herds and put into destination pastures awaiting the heifers.

Archer took his place, as did his brothers. Graham was the point, in the forward position, steering the herd. Cooper was the swing, riding on the side of the herd while Ash took the drag position, picking up stragglers and then he toggled between flank, keeping the herd from becoming to wide, and a second swing.

They had trained cattle dogs with them. The dogs could cut a cow from the herd better than most men. They also acted as back-up drags, picking up any stragglers and getting them back in line. It took several hours to get the herds cut and driven into holding pastures until the next day when they would reintroduce them to the bull's pasture.

"Damn." Cooper took off his hat, used his bandana from around his neck to wipe the sweat off of his face.

"I damn well second that," Ash said, taking a long draw off his canteen.

Graham had headed out to inspect the fence lines. He returned with a grim expression.

"They pulled down half an acre." He told them. "We've got to get supplies and get this fixed."

"I'll head into town," Ash said.

They all gathered in one spot, sitting on their horses, catching their breath.

Archer was thinking about Vicky. He found this to be a rather regular happening. As if his brothers read his mind, Ash said, "Don't get ticked off, Archer."

"I already am," Archer said, only half kidding.

"I'm just showing concern," Ash said.

Archer shook his head with a sigh. "Am I ever going to outrun the shadow of my past?"

Cooper said to Ash and Graham. "You guys just need to back off and support him."

"We will support him. Of course we will," Ash said. "But does that mean we can't have a conversation?"

"And I don't want to go through it again," Archer said. "I get to make mistakes in my life. I'm the youngest, I get it. But I'm still a grown man."

Cooper and Ash exchanged glances and then looked at Graham. Graham shook his head. "I don't have room to preach."

"You guys don't have to like it but I do expect you to support me in this. I'm marrying Vicky Woodson," he said, picking up his reins. "That's my final word on that subject."

"Hey, Archer!" Ash said. "If Vicky is who you want, then she's who we want for you."

"She's who I want."

"Then let's just squash this thing and congratulate the baby of the family."

Archer cracked a smile. "You were doing great until that last remark."

Archer rode on with his brothers, feeling a weight lifted off his shoulders. He could forge his own path fighting the gale force winds that came in the form of his three older brothers if the situation required, but to have their support just paved the way to an easier transition for Vicky, for him, and their child.

"How do you want your hair?" Cassie asked, brushing out her freshly washed hair. They were trying out different styles for the wedding.

"I don't know." She stared at her reflection in the bathroom mirror. "Something that won't emphasize how round my face is now."

"Victoria Woodson! Quit being mean to yourself! You look beautiful. You've always been beautiful. And you will be a beautiful bride tomorrow."

As she entered her fifth month of pregnancy, the feeling of being bloated and sluggish had just materialized. Jeans were now nothing but a fond memory, and it would soon be time for maternity clothing.

"How about if we braid the sides of your hair and leave the rest down?" Cassie asked. "Your hair is so thick and shiny."

"For now," she said sullenly.

That drew a pointed look from her best friend. "What do you mean?"

"Hormones," Vicky said. "Lots of pregnant women lose their hair during pregnancy."

Now Cassie was frowning at her. "That's it! We are breaking out the ice cream."

"Alright."

Vicky followed her into the kitchen and sat down at the table, elbows resting on the top, chin in both of her hands. Cassie brought over the ice cream, two tablespoons, a determined expression on her face.

"So, talk to me. What's going on?"

Vicky dug out a giant helping of ice cream, ate it and immediately felt better. That was the power of mint-chocolate-chip.

With a second full load of ice cream on her spoon, she said, "I don't know if I can go through with it, Cass. I really don't know."

Cassie cocked her head to the side with raised eyebrows. "Do you mean that you can't go through with the marriage that takes place less than twenty-four hours from now?"

Mouthful of ice cream, she nodded.

"Why?"

"Because I am scared, I am confused, my brain doesn't know what to think, my heart is getting attached to Archer and I just can't. I'm keeping another huge secret from just about everyone in my life *again*! My keeping a huge secret is the very reason I am about to marry Archer, a man who is my friend, but is he my true love? I don't know. Am I his true love? I don't think so. We are just too different."

"Okay," Cassie said. "A lot to unpack here."

"And, speaking of packing, I'm supposed to move into Archer's cabin after the wedding. He took me there. It's very tranquil and lovely and uber masculine in the middle of nowhere." She waved her spoon in the air. "He wants me to decorate. He's given me carte blanche!"

"How dare he! Off with his head!" Cassie tried to tease her into a better mood.

She frowned at her best friend.

"Okay," Cassie said. "I'll be serious. Bottom line. Yes, you are keeping a secret—the marriage is one of convenience—not the first time that has happened in the West."

"I'm not a mail-order bride, Cassie."

"If you are or aren't, is it really anyone's business?" her friend asked pointedly. "No. It's not. It's between you and Archer and that's it. This isn't a repeat of the stolen money, Vicky."

"I hid the money to protect my mother and now I'm marrying Archer to protect my baby."

"You were a child trying to save her family, covering up a crime. You are a woman now, making a woman's decision to put her child first."

Vicky liked Cassie's version of the recent events and her decision to accept Archer's proposal.

"But I'll be lying to his family. They're such lovely people. I don't want to hurt them unnecessarily."

"Trust me, Vicky, the Callahan family is tough as nails. Marriages break up all the time for any number of reasons."

Vicky had told Cassie the two main reasons for wanting to back out of the wedding, but the third reason was the one that was giving her the most grief.

"Why do I feel like you are holding something back?" Cassie asked her.

"Because I'm holding something back."

Her friend waited.

"I think..." She started, paused, and then restarted. "I think that I may be developing some..."

"Feelings for Archer?"

Vicky nodded.

"I can see why that would be scary," Cassie said. "After all, that happened to me with Graham. I didn't know if I was the only one to catch feelings. It felt horrible, quite honestly."

"I remember."

"Well, Graham and I both think that Archer may be catching some feelings for you as well."

"You do?"

Cassie nodded. "We do."

"Oh."

Vicky felt so mixed up, but her friend's words did give her some comfort. She had projected years down the road to a day when Archer found his real bride-to-be and how jealous Vicky would feel. Maybe, just maybe, Archer was feeling nervous about his feelings for her without knowing how soon she would walk out of his life, baby in tow.

"Vicky, marry Archer. If I didn't think this was the right move, I would have tied you to that chair to stop you from doing it."

Vicky laughed at the thought.

"But I don't feel that way. This is the right thing for you. And not just because I want you to stay in Tenacity." Cassie reached over for her hand and squeezed it. "Answer this question. Is marrying Archer the best decision for your child right now?"

Without hesitation, Vicky said, "Yes."

"Then, that's your answer. Right?"

"Right."

That was the moment when they looked down at the container of ice cream.

"We just hoovered half a gallon," Cassie said.

"We can't be trusted." Vicky nodded. "Good thing I don't have to be zipped up into a dress with a corset."

"Amen."

The next morning, Vicky was at Nothin' New with Cassie and May Bell. The store was closed, and it was the perfect spot for Cassie and May Bell to help her get ready for her eleven o'clock nuptials. Before Cassie was to work on her hair and makeup, May Bell helped her into a vintage wedding gown that she had been holding back in her own personal stash for just the right person and just the right moment.

"May Bell." Vicky studied her reflection. "It's so beautiful. How can I possibly thank you?"

"You can thank me by having a wonderful life with a wonderful future. I don't know anyone more deserving than you."

The V-necked dress was made of delicate lace, with dainty pearl buttons on the back and long sleeves that had volume at the elbow. There was enough room in the A-line dress for her very rounded belly and, because of her pregnancy, for the first time, she was able to fill out the bustline.

Vicky turned and kissed May Bell on the cheek, then hugged her. "Thank you so much, May Bell, for everything. Absolutely everything."

Chapter Nine

Wearing her lovely vintage dress, Vicky walked into Castillo's feeling like a beautiful bride. As a nod to her husband-to-be, she had donned a pair of white cowgirl boots, and discovered that she liked them very much. Cassie had worked overtime to turn the restaurant into a romantic wedding venue. The lighting was low with spotlights here and there, situated to catch the bride and groom in the best light for the pictures. A photographer was not available on such short notice, so Cassie had tasked all of the guests with the job of capturing the wedding from their phones. After the wedding, Cassie would select the best of the best and create a keepsake photo album.

Vicky and Cassie, the maid of honor, stopped in the foyer and waited for the ceremony to begin. At that time, the music would begin to play, the double doors that led from the foyer into the dining area would open and she'd walk down to the custom-made pergola that was fashioned from twisted wood decorated with sunflowers.

"Ooh." Vicky felt queasy, and her baby was kicking and changing positions, which only made her feel like she had to make a quick pit stop at the ladies'. But the thought of accidentally dropping the hem of her dress in the bowl or accidentally getting a smudge of dirt on any part of the dress stopped her.

"'Ooh' what?" her best friend asked.

"I feel sick to my stomach."

"Nerves-sick or sick-sick?"

Vicky shook her head. "Not sure."

"Buck up! I have been running on fumes for a week setting this up."

"I know. You're the best."

"Victoria Woodson, I'm telling you right now, this wedding is happening."

Vicky closed her eyes, breathed in deeply and then let it out slowly. In the meantime, Graham, Archer's obvious choice for a best man, poked his head in the door. "Everyone's seated. Are we going?"

"Ooh." Vicky put her hands on her belly, mentally begging her baby to just settle down and let her get through what was deliberately meant to be a quick ceremony, just like their relationship.

"Tell them to turn on the music," Cassie said.

Graham gave her a thumb's-up and went to do that bidding.

"Are you better?" Cassie asked her, sincere concern in her eyes.

Vicky swallowed hard several times and nodded. "Yes. I've got to get some rest, my precious," she said to her baby. "I'm getting married."

Cassie hugged her tightly and she hugged her back just as tightly. "You'll be fine. After all you've been through, this will be a piece of cake."

The music started and Graham joined them in the foyer. Offering his arm to his fiancée, the best man and maid of honor walked ahead of Vicky, and then she followed. She decided to have her brother give her away to Archer. Yes, her father was attending, and she loved him truly. But his abuse of power when he was mayor had put a rift between them. She hoped that someday they would be able to find their way back to the strong father-daughter bond they'd once had. For now, she was happy to just have him there.

Holding a bouquet of sunflowers, Vicky walked slowly toward the pergola while Cassie and Graham took their places. For her, Archer was the only person she could see. The rest of the room was a blur. Standing tall and confident, Archer was dressed in dark-wash jeans, shined-up cowboy boots, and a nicely pressed button-down shirt with the agate bolo tie May Bell had given him.

When she reached him, he reached out his hand to her and she took it.

"You look…" Archer paused. "You are stunning."

She smiled at him and held his two hands in hers. Their hands were both sweaty, so at least they weren't going it alone.

"You look handsome."

He smiled at her with a wink. "In ten minutes, I'll be all yours."

It didn't matter in the moment that that wasn't true. Not that she thought he would be romancing other ladies while they were married. Archer wasn't like that. He was a stand-up guy, just like his brother Graham. This all *felt* real, and she had always had, from the beginning, difficulty keeping reality and fiction separate.

"Dearly beloved…" The justice of the peace began the ceremony.

Her knees were shaking, her body was trembling, her palms even sweatier now. Oddly, looking into Archer's green eyes worked to calm her down. The vows were simple and went by in a blink of an eye. Next, they were exchanging rings—unembellished yellow-gold bands.

"By the power vested in me," said the officiant, "I now pronounce you husband and wife. Mr. Callahan, you may kiss your bride."

This was their first kiss. It was possible that they would never have another.

He whispered in her ear, "May I?"

She nodded, and when their lips touched, quickly, gently,

the room was filled with claps and whistles. That kiss had been tender and perfect and only served to increase her respect for her new husband. Archer offered his arm and together they stepped forward as husband and wife. Her father met them and gave her an emotional bear hug. Archer offered his hand to Mr. Woodson, and her father shook it. She had never seen her dad so filled with raw emotion.

"Thank you for inviting me, Button," her father said, using his nickname for her for as long as she could remember.

"I love you, Dad. Nothing can ever change that."

Then her mother came to her and there was such pride and sorrow in June's eyes that it almost—*almost*—made her cry. "You are the most beautiful bride, Victoria."

"Thank you, Mom." She hugged her mother, long and hard, knowing that she would be able to support her because Archer had agreed to be her husband.

"And, Archer," June said to Vicky's husband of no more than five minutes. "Thank you. What a blessing."

June hadn't asked about the paternity of the child she was carrying, and Vicky knew that her mom didn't really care at this point. This was her first grandchild and June was eager to spend any time she could with the little one in her daughter's belly.

"Thank you, Mrs. Woodson," Archer said respectfully.

The next thirty minutes was spent circulating through the room, greeting their guests while the staff of Castillo's began to fill the buffet with all of the favorites from the menu. By the time they found their way back to their seats at the front of the room, where everyone could see them, Vicky was both exhausted and exhilarated.

Archer leaned in close to her. "How are you holding up, Mrs. Callahan?"

Two weeks ago, she had accepted a date with Archer Callahan, and now she was back at Castillo's wearing a wedding dress and a simple gold wedding band. She was now, incredibly and unexpectedly, Mrs. Victoria Woodson-Callahan.

"I'm holding up very well, Mr. Callahan. Thank you for asking." She leaned her head toward his. "How about you?"

"I feel like I'm at the right place, at the right time, doing the right thing."

Vicky was about to respond when Cassie stood up, started to clap and chant, "Kiss, kiss, kiss, kiss."

"Let's not disappoint our audience," Archer said.

"We shouldn't," Vicky said with a grin.

When their lips touched for a second time, it was with more intensity than their chaste wedding kiss. Vicky had never felt anything as *stirring* as Archer's lips upon hers. She didn't care if it lasted all night, but Archer ended it all too soon. This seal-the-deal kiss would most likely be the last one. It was sweet, sweet and it left her wanting to linger in that kiss.

After the crowd died down when they kissed as requested, Vicky said to Archer, "Cassie is a troublemaker. Have you noticed that?"

Archer smiled at her. "I've picked up on that. But, in her defense, her trouble is usually *good* trouble."

After the plates had been cleared, and right before the cake-cutting, Graham and Cassie, filling the roles of best man and maid of honor, stood to give toasts to the newlyweds.

"Archer." Graham held up his glass. "I've always loved you like a brother."

"I *am* your brother!"

"Oh! That's right. You are." The crowd laughed as Graham continued. "You are a great guy, Archer. You've got a good heart, always ready to take in anything with a broken wing. You're a true friend and brother. The only thing left for me to do is to tell you that I love you and I wish you the best in this next chapter of your life. And, Vicky, you are more than just

Cassie's best friend. You are a part of the Callahan family any way you slice it. To the bride and groom!"

The one line in Graham's speech that struck a sour note for Vicky was the broken-wing comment. Was that what this was all about? Archer wanting to rescue her? They had discussed this. She had told him that she wasn't broken or in need of rescuing. For the moment, she stored that in the back of her mind for later because Cassie now held the floor.

"Vicky." Cassie started with an emotional tone in her voice. "I've known you my whole entire life and I want to know you for the rest of it. I am so fortunate to have you as my best friend. You are kind, sweet, so smart and loving. I love you."

Vicky put her hands over heart and said, "I love you."

"And, Archer…" Cassie continued. "When you asked me if I thought asking out our Vicky was a good idea, I had no idea that I would be standing here toasting the two of you at your wedding."

The crowd laughed. How could they not?

"Take care of her, Archer."

"I will," Archer promised.

After the toasts, she joined Archer at a nearby table to cut the wedding cakes in their favorite flavors—red velvet and cream cheese frosting for her and carrot cake for him.

While their guests looked on, they held the knife together and cut one slice of each cake and, as they had discussed and planned, fed each other one bite of the ones they loved the most.

"Oh, my word," Vicky said of the cake May Bell had made. It had been Emil's favorite and now it was hers.

"She can bake the heck out of cake, can't she?"

"Yes." Vicky went to May Bell, hugged her and thanked her for the wonderful cake.

"You're welcome, honey," May Bell said. "I sure do feel my dearly departed husband Emil. Lord, I do miss that man. He's here, though. I feel him," May Bell said. "He would not let a little thing like death stop him from eating that cake!"

Archer felt tired but triumphant. His plan to solve Vicky's problems and keep her in Tenacity, where he truly believed that she belonged, had been successful. And it didn't matter to him one way or another if folks in town didn't believe their union was anything more than a farce. Not his problem. With one exception. Brent Woodson. Vicky's brother had come up to the table, hugged his sister, then stuck his hand out for him to shake. Archer had stood, as was proper, and shaken Brent's hand with a firm grip. Under his breath, Brent had said to him, "I don't know what's going on here with all of this foolishness, Callahan, but it would be best if you tread lightly. My sister's been through enough. Too much. Don't you make things worse."

"I make this promise to you now, Brent. I will take care of her. And her baby."

"I hope so. Time will tell." And with that, the conversation with Brent ended abruptly.

It took Archer a moment to shake off Brent's words. Not everyone was going to be on board with their decision. It was understandable, of course, but his mission would remain unchanged. Focus on marriage to Vicky and be there for her child.

"Thank you so much, Mr. and Mrs. Castillo," Archer said, handing Yolanda his bank card to pay for the food and the use of the space, adding a sizable tip.

Yolanda looked at the receipt, her eyes opening wide. "Are you sure of this?"

"Yes. Your staff did an excellent job."

"Thank you. We were so pleased that you gave us the honor of hosting your wedding."

Pablo grinned. "You must come back here, every year, for your anniversary!"

Archer shook the owner's hand. "We will. Every year."

With Vicky by his side, they stopped in the foyer, thanked their guests and the Castillos one more time, then he whisked his bride away.

"It was like a real wedding," Vicky said as she took her place in the passenger seat.

Archer laughed. "That's because it *was* a real wedding. We are officially hitched."

Vicky tried to stifle a yawn as she said, "You know what I mean."

He started the engine. "If you're tired, just lean back the seat all the way and I'll wake you when we get there."

"You don't mind?"

"Not at all."

Vicky moaned in pleasure as she laid back, closed her eyes and then felt the seat heater begin to wrap her in a comfortable warmth. "This is a little slice of heaven."

As he drove, Archer looked over at his sleeping bride frequently, perhaps his way of mentally pinching himself. He had actually married this lovely woman. It was bizarre and impulsive. It didn't make good sense, he knew that. But he felt something unique and powerful for Vicky Woodson. Correction: Victoria Woodson-Callahan. It was magnetic between them, an observable, unmistakable chemistry that was pointed out by many guests at the wedding, even the skeptics. With the soft, rhythmic breathing of his wife and the dark road laid out before him, Archer had some time to think about what had brought him to this moment. He realized that what he felt for Vicky went beyond liking her as a friend. He'd tried that on for size and it just didn't fit.

"It's gotta be love," Archer said aloud.

Waking, Vicky turned her head toward him with a "Hmm?"

"Nothing. Go back to sleep."

"Mmm. Okay."

So, what was holding him back?

Was it fear of rejection because she was the one woman who really mattered and her rejection would cut deep in a way that other women, fun and in abundance, had not?

Yes.

Was it fear of repeating a mistake from his past that had haunted him for years?

Of course.

Was he worried that Vicky didn't return his feelings?

Absolutely. She was always bringing up the end of their marriage as a certainty.

He wanted to touch her, hold her, kiss her, and breathe in the scent of her hair and feel her skin next to his. But Vicky had pulled away from him more often than not. The last thing he wanted was to overstep a boundary in *that* department.

Bottom line, he was all mixed up.

He pulled onto the property, shut off the engine, and lightly touched her arm to wake her.

"Vicky."

"Hmm?"

"We're here."

Vicky opened her eyes half-mast, pushed the button to lift the seat into its upright position, and blinked sleepily, yawning loudly before she focused on the landscape around her.

"Where are we?" she asked.

"Thunder Canyon Resort."

"Are you serious?"

"We have to have a honeymoon, don't we?"

He could see her eyes turn watery, as if she was about to cry.

"Happy tears?"

Vicky nodded and put her finger at the corners of her eyes to stop those tears from having a chance to fall. "I never expected this."

"Good," he said. "That's why I did it."

"What about clothing? Toothbrushes?"

"All packed." He opened his door. "And don't worry. I didn't rummage through your underwear drawer. Cassie packed yours."

"Good." Vicky smiled as he went around to lend her a hand out of the truck.

He still couldn't get over how beautiful she looked in her white dress with her mussed dark red hair framing her face. His gaze swept over her from head to toe.

"Nice boots," he said.

She smiled, picked up the skirt of her dress to show them off. "I love them. I really think I need more."

He pulled out their suitcases from the covered truck bed and put them on the ground.

"See?" Archer asked her. "What did I tell you? You've got some cowgirl hiding in there just waiting to break free."

"Do you know what, Mr. Callahan?"

"What's that?"

"You just might be right."

Vicky walked into the honeymoon suite at Thunder Canyon Resort with a feeling of wonder. Yes, their family had been fortunate to travel and stay at nice hotels. But this honeymoon suite was way beyond her experience.

She waited until the valet unloaded their luggage and wedding gifts and left, then turned to Archer. "Archer, what have you done?"

"I made a reservation."

"But this is too much!" Vicky gestured to the enormous living room, kitchenette, grand bedroom and wrap-around balcony. "We don't need all of this to convince people our marriage is real."

Archer took off his hat, ran his fingers through his hair. "Newlyweds go on a honeymoon, Vicky."

"Well," Vicky said, her arms crossed, "not everyone can afford one."

"We can. I've been saving up for something special."

"There isn't any 'we' in this, Archer. I live in a tiny apartment above a grocery store." She clipped coupons and was a sales-rack aficionado.

He walked over to her with a genuinely confused expression. "Why are you angry?"

"I'm not!"

"Yes, you are. I thought you would be pleased."

She was pleased. And overwhelmed. And exhausted. And confused. She was everything all at once.

"I am grateful," she said. "For this. For everything. I just don't want you to waste your money on a marriage that hasn't been designed to last."

She saw Archer's jaw tighten—in frustration, she imagined—and she felt guilty that she had already gotten them off on the wrong foot.

"Do you want to go back to Tenacity?" Archer had his hands in his front pockets and a guarded look on his face. "Just tell me what you want."

She walked to him, took his hands out of his pockets, and held them in hers. "I—" She started, stopped, and then restarted. "I don't want you to regret this."

"I won't."

"How do you know?"

"Because I want this for myself as much as for you."

Now, Vicky was stumped. She said nothing, just looked up at him, searching his green eyes for some hint to what he meant by that.

Archer sighed, ran his hand over the stubble on his face. "I'd be lying if I didn't say all of the attention you and your family draw in town didn't bother me. Sometimes it does. I needed a place— No..." He pointed to each of them several times. "*We* needed a place where we could be away from prying eyes, rest, relax, and figure out a game plan for our return to Tenacity."

Chapter Ten

Vicky was floating in a soaker bathtub that was bigger than the size of her entire bathroom. Covered by fragrant bubbles, she felt as if every muscle in her body relaxed as the warm water did its best work. It tickled her that her belly looked like an island rising up from the ocean around it.

"Riley," she said to her baby, "I love you so much. I can't wait to see your precious face."

At her next appointment, she was far enough along to find out the gender. Now, all along, she had been determined to keep the gender a secret until the very end. But Cassie and Archer had been wearing her down. Cassie was beside herself because she wanted to throw a gender reveal party in the worst way. Lately, she had been pondering it. Perhaps it would be fun to have a party to celebrate her baby. Girl or boy, the baby was already perfect.

She submerged herself a few moments longer and then she stepped out onto the plush bath mat, dried herself off with a giant bath towel, rubbed a luxurious, thick cream on her arms and legs and belly, then slipped into the softest robe and slippers she had ever encountered. She did a quick pickup of the bathroom and then emerged a very happy, very spoiled, woman.

She half expected to find Archer sprawled on the king-sized bed—the only bed—but he wasn't there. She walked out into the living room to find him on one of the couches. He was still dressed, boots propped up on one armrest, hat over his face.

"Archer." She poked him gently with her pointer finger. "Archer."

Nothing. No reaction at all.

Then she poked him a bit harder. "Archer."

What in the world?

This time, she shook him and said his name louder.

Third time was a charm. He sprung up, his hat falling at her feet, startled.

"Yeah?" He felt around for his hat. She handed it to him.

"Where are you going to sleep?"

He looked at her like she was making no sense at all.

"Right here." He gestured to the couch behind him, where he'd been doing just that a moment ago.

While in the tub, Vicky had thought through the fact that she would be sharing a hotel room with a man she had only known for two weeks. Her conclusion? Things could get super awkward. Luckily there were two bathrooms in the suite, so that concern was handled. But one bed? That was a quandary.

"No," Vicky said. "You can't sleep on the couch. You're too tall."

"I'm fine, Vic," he said groggily. "I've slept on hard ground out on the ranch.

"That may be, and that's fine when you're at the ranch. While we are here, we will share the bed like two grown-ups. And if you give me even one ounce of resistance, I'm calling the front desk, and I will have them move us to that 'adjoining room' situation you mentioned."

"I don't want to move," he grumbled. "This is a pullout if I need it."

"Those are horrible even in a nice place like this. The ball is in your court, Archer. Two choices, each with a move in it. You either move from here into the bedroom or move to adjoining rooms."

Archer frowned and then he strode to the bedroom, not saying a word. He swept away the heart-shaped towels propped up in front of the pillows, yanked off his boots, took his bolo tie off and then ripped off his shirt and tossed it in a nearby chair. He flopped onto the comforter on the right side of the bed, pounded his pillows with his fist and shut his eyes.

"Now don't go thinking that you can take advantage of me," Archer mumbled. "Just because we're married doesn't mean you can have your way with me."

She laughed. "Don't worry, Mr. Callahan, your chastity is safe with me."

If she had expected more teasing or anything resembling a conversation at all with her new husband, she would have been sorely disappointed. One minute after he had said his last word to her, he was snoring lightly.

She looked at him, amazed. "I would give anything to fall asleep that quickly," she said to herself.

She turned off the lights on the night tables and then tiptoed into the living room, shutting the door behind her. She found the remote control for the massive TV, settled in a comfy place on the couch and channel surfed. Her mind just wouldn't settle on anything to watch. So, she did what she always did when she couldn't sleep or had a problem or just wanted to talk for the heck of it, she called Cassie.

"Were you surprised?" her friend asked as soon as she answered.

"Completely. I fell asleep and woke up in Thunder Canyon."

Vicky took her friend on a video tour of the honeymoon suite, including the sexy cowboy in her bed.

"It's amazing," Cassie said. "I know where I'll want to go for our honeymoon."

"For sure."

"Okay. Dish."

"Not much to dish." Vicky leaned back on the comfy, extra-deep couch. "I do think we had our first fight of our marriage."

Cassie laughed. "You guys do everything at warp speed."

"I suppose we do," she said with a tired smile. The day was beginning to catch up with her. "I just want to thank you for everything. The ceremony, the reception, and packing for this trip. I love you."

"I love you," Cassie said. "Now, try to get some rest. And, for the love of mint-chocolate-chip ice cream, enjoy the ride a little!"

"I will. I promise."

Vicky wished Cassie good-night and then opened her suitcase, grateful to see her favorite pregnancy nightie that said Baby on Board with an arrow pointing to her belly. Whenever she put that gown on, with a pair of footy socks, she felt ready for bed. She washed her face, brushed her teeth and then looked at the sleeping rancher in her bed.

"Buckle up, Riley. We Woodsons do not live ordinary lives."

As gently as she could, she lifted the covers and slid in. The pillows were super fluffy and there was one for her head and one to cuddle with. Her mind was racing, and Riley moving felt like butterflies inside of her rounding belly. Vicky was able to drift away in a cloud made of high-thread-count cotton sheets, a super-soft mattress, and feathery pillows made for the gods. It was so perfect. The only thing that could top this moment? A real marriage and a real husband.

Archer awakened on top of the comforter, spooning his wife-in-name-only, with his nose buried in her hair that smelled as fresh as an ocean breeze. Almost immediately he noticed that another part of his body was wide awake as well.

He cursed under his breath, rolled over, and made a beeline for his suitcase, grabbing toiletries and clean clothes. Of course, his body was going to react. It would be darn strange if it hadn't. Vicky was a beautiful woman. And her body, which was blooming from the pregnancy, was appealing to him. He couldn't have foreseen that because he'd never been with a woman who was pregnant. However, this wasn't just anyone. This was the lovely Miss Woodson, and he felt all kinds of attraction to her.

Archer showered, shaved, got dressed in his regular jeans, a T-shirt, and put on his boots. He ran a comb through his wet hair and then studied his reflection. "She's not the lovely Miss Woodson anymore, Arch," he reminded himself again. "She's the lovely Mrs. Woodson-Callahan."

He hunted down a room service menu and ordered a wide variety of items. One of them had to be right for Vicky. The food had just arrived when his bride appeared, wearing a robe and slippers, her auburn hair tousled in the sexiest of ways.

"Good morning," she said.

"Hungry?"

"Famished."

Vicky padded over and joined him at a table that could easily seat ten.

"Wow," she said. "That's a lot of food."

"I didn't know what you'd like."

Instead of digging in, his bride picked up a plate and then asked him what he would like. He was caught off guard but named items and then she handed the full plate to him.

"Thank you," he said.

"Thank you, Archer."

After spooning some scrambled eggs, grits, and toast onto her plate, she sat down. She polished off the eggs, then went back for some more.

"What's on the agenda?" she asked. "Do I need to get dressed or is this a bathrobe and pj's kind of day?"

"I've got some things planned for you."

Vicky took a bite of toast, chewed, and then asked, "What?"

"I just picked a bunch of stuff. I figured one of the things I picked would be a winner."

"Like the food."

"Exactly. Like with the food," he said, feeling the mood shift back to his desired direction. "Let me see here." Archer scrolled through his texts. "I signed you up for a massage with hot stones, a mud bath—that sounds weird, but they told me that it was a bestseller. I do have mud right there on the ranch, if you find you like it. A facial, a cut and a blow-dry."

"Thank you, Archer. I mean it. Thank you. But it's too much."

"My dear wife," Archer said plainly. "It makes me happy to see you happy. Shouldn't that be enough right now?"

Vicky sat back down, stared at him while shaking her head in disbelief. She reached for his hand, and he liked the feel of her delicate hand in his. "That's the nicest thing anyone has ever said to me. How can I say 'no' after that?"

"You can't." He grinned with a wink.

Vicky was at the end of her spa day, and she felt like the most pampered woman in the world. Never in her life had she experienced the generosity that Archer had shown her. She realized she'd judged him based only on his handsome appearance. Yes, he could be rough around the edges, and he certainly had a sizable streak of macho, red-blooded cowboy ego. But instead of making him less appealing to her, she found all of that rough-and-tumble cowboy with a romantic heart very appealing. And it wasn't just her mind that registered that fact. So had her body.

Oh, her body. She had read that some pregnant women experienced an increased libido, particularly in their second trimester. After last night, her body wanted Archer. And when she had awakened to find her husband's arm wrapped tightly around her, his body following the curve of her body, she had felt Archer's sexual desire for her. She'd tried to figure out how to untangle herself from him but, when he'd begun to stir, she'd shut her eyes and feigned sleep until he'd left the bedroom.

That experience with Archer had switched her on and she didn't have any way to shut it back off.

While she was sitting in the rock-salt room in a wonderful lounge chair, sipping on a seltzer with strawberries, she called Cassie.

"I know," Cassie said after Vicky had recounted the spa day Archer had arranged for her. "The Callahan men. They look like they're going to be overly obnoxious alpha males with big trucks and even bigger egos. But beneath that exterior, there is a—"

"Romantic," Vicky said.

"A romantic." She gave a small sigh, then asked, "Anything to report from last night?"

Vicky looked around to see if anyone was in hearing distance. Softly, she said, "When I woke up, Archer was spooning with me."

"Okay. Fill me in. I'm here for it."

Vicky brought Cassie up to speed. It wasn't a surprise that she found her husband to be attractive. It was like suddenly finding a Hemsworth brother in her bed. Fit, lean, big biceps, strong shoulders, beautiful pecs with some chest hair that made her want to run her fingers through it. Great bone structure, and those lips… To die for. Scarred up a bit, reminding her that he was a man who was daring and got his hands dirty on the regular. And now, fortunately and unfortunately, she had confirmed—with hard evidence—that her husband found her to be attractive as well.

"Honestly, I kind of want to jump his bones."

Cassie laughed along with her. "Why don't you, then?"

"Consummate the marriage?" Vicky recoiled at the thought. "I can't."

"Why not?"

"I—I—I don't want to get more attached than I already am."

"I get that," her bestie said. "But maybe just leave that door open."

"You mean friends with benefits? I don't want to mislead him. Or myself for that matter."

"What if this friendship turns into something more?"

"I don't know," Vicky said truthfully. "There are too many variables to even make a logical guess. We barely know each other and now we're married."

"Well, I'm going to keep the faith. Wouldn't it be amazing if we both ended up with Callahan men?"

"Best friends and sisters-in-law?"

"Perfect," Cassie said. "Okay. Let me go. Keep me in the loop."

"You know I will."

Archer went to the resort bar. The place was crowded, with people milling about, while several TV screens showed different sporting events. Periodically, he would feel a weight on his left ring finger, drawing his attention to the gold wedding band. It felt like it was always meant to be there.

As he ordered his next beer, Vicky texted. She wrote that she was heading his way.

"How are you liking your stay?" the bartender asked him.

Archer held up his left hand. "Honeymoon."

"Nice, brother," the bartender said. "Congrats."

"You married?"

"No. No. Not for me. I did try it once or twice. But, no." The bartender laughed. "Let me know if you need anything else."

"Thank you." Archer took a swig of his beer and then spotted two people he recognized from Tenacity.

"No rest for the weary," he muttered.

He had sunglasses on, but he thought that they had clocked him. When Vicky arrived, looking relaxed and dewy and happy, he stood up, took her face in his hands and he kissed her like a man would kiss his newlywed wife.

After the kiss, he whispered in her ear, "Tenacity folk. Twelve o'clock."

Vicky gave a tiny nod then kissed him again, holding on to his shoulders, and when the kiss was broken, she gazed up at him with those incredible, sultry blue eyes and said, "I love you."

Archer felt like he had just been knocked right between the eyes. He knew she was playing a role. He knew that she was putting on a show for the people staring at them from the other side of the bar. It made him feel a sort of way that was foreign, unnerving, and downright confusing. How could this woman make him feel all twisted up inside?

Vicky took a seat next to him, leaning in his direction, her hand resting on his thigh.

"Can I have a virgin piña colada?" she asked the bartender.

"Coming right up." When he delivered the drink, he announced to the other patrons that they were on their honeymoon.

The crowd in the bar yelled congrats, whistled, and clapped, and Archer couldn't have planned better proof for the Tenacity couple who went on their way once they had their drinks.

"That was close," Vicky said.

"That was a warning that we need to behave like newlyweds everywhere we go once we're back home."

"It was."

Vicky caught his eye and held his attention when she said, "Thank you, Archer. No one has ever pampered me like you have.

"Well." He cleared his throat, trying to stop his body from reacting to her hand on his thigh. "You're welcome."

Archer was relieved when Vicky took her hand away. He was really irritated with his body for behaving like a teenage boy in the back of a truck getting to second base for the first time.

"Are you hungry?" he asked.

"Honestly, I'm still pretty stuffed from breakfast."

"Back to the room, then?"

"Yes. I'm kind of freaked out that we ran into Tenacity folks here."

"Yeah. Me, too."

On the way up to the room, Archer couldn't stop thinking about how Vicky felt in his arms. The scent of her hair. The silkiness of her skin. He did have to admit that he felt *concerned* about making love to a woman who was pregnant; he had certainly never considered the desirability of a pregnant woman in his life. But when it came to Vicky, her being pregnant didn't change the fact that he wanted to make love to his wife, fake or real. Was this going to be a constant battle for the rest of their marriage? They had never truly discussed an exit plan; they had only been focused on the entry.

"After you," he said when the elevator doors opened.

Together, they walked to their suite and, what had become a habit for them since their first date, she hooked her arm with his and it made him feel *closer* to her, and he liked it. Together they entered their sanctuary. He put the Do Not Disturb sign on the door handle and then bolted the door shut.

"We can shut out the world here," Vicky said, kicking off her shoes.

"Damn straight."

There was an odd silence between them as they both looked around the room. What were they supposed to do now? As well as they'd clicked from the jump, he suddenly realized that they simply didn't know each other much at all. What did she like to do in her spare time? Was she a night owl? Did she eat in bed? These were the things that most couples found out when they were dating. They had only had two true dates: Castillo's and the dinosaur dig.

"What now?" Vicky asked, looking at him with the same look in her eyes that he felt inside.

"We could watch a movie. Or sit on the balcony."

"Balcony first. Then a movie and popcorn."

"I like how you think."

They opened the sliding wall that folded in on itself like an accordion. Archer took off his shirt and sat with the sun warm on his skin.

"This is awkward." Vicky put voice to his thoughts.

"It is that."

"It will get better. Don't you think?"

"In time," he agreed, wanting to dampen the worry he heard in her voice. "We just have to be patient."

Chapter Eleven

The second night of their honeymoon, Vicky felt more comfortable sharing a room with Archer. He was like a stone thrown in the pond that produced only a few ripples. In sharp contrast to her husband's public persona was his private one. In private, he was more relaxed and more reflective. He was a history buff, and liked to devour anything from the ancient world, particularly Egypt and the pyramids. Archer also loved programs on the universe. What he loved the most was music. And it wasn't just country—yes, there was a lot of that—but he listened to heavy metal, some alternative, and a couple of favorite rappers. Archer also confided that he had teared up at the end of the movie *The Notebook*.

"Okay." Vicky sat cross-legged on the couch, which gave her growing belly a nice, comfortable cradle. "I think that Riley may have just attempted to kick me," she reported with a sense of wonder.

"Is that the name you have chosen?"

"Yes. Riley Cassandra for a girl, and Riley Brent for a boy."

"I like that."

"Thank you. Me, too." After a moment she said, "I think she's hungry."

"That makes two of us."

Vicky smiled. "Three of us, actually."

"Room service?"

"Yes, please."

When room service arrived, they sat at the table, enjoying the meal. They had already decided that they should have a horror movie marathon with popcorn and root beer. While they were clearing off the table, she got a text message from Cassie.

"Geez," she said, looking at her phone.

"What now?"

"We've made the *Tenacity Tattler* again."

Archer walked over and looked at the photo of them kissing in the resort bar. The article was accompanied by a picture and a caption: Newlyweds Canoodling at Thunder Canyon Resort.

"It had to be that older couple that spotted us," she said. "Who, in this century, uses the word *canoodling*?"

Archer went quiet. Was it getting to him? This spotlight that she had carried in one way or another all of her life. First as the daughter of a powerful mayor, and now, as a scandalous "trainwreck" who drew the often-unwelcome attention of strangers.

"Do you know what I think?" Archer finally said.

"Tell me."

"If it's a show they want, let's give them the best darn show any of them have ever seen."

"Meaning?"

"When we are out in public, here or in Tenacity, we act as if we're totally into each other."

"PDA."

"Always. Hugging, kissing, holding on tight."

"Okay. Why not? This picture is working in our favor."

"Exactly," Archer said. "That's my point. Why the heck are we hiding up here when we can be out enjoying our honeymoon? Let them take all of the pictures they want."

She walked over to him and held out her hand. "Deal?" she asked.

He shook her hand. "Heck, yeah."

* * *

The next two days, also their last two days of the honeymoon, they toured the resort, taking long walks together, restaurant hopping, all the while holding on tight to each other, holding hands, whispering sweet nothings, and kissing. Lots of kissing. And even though they hadn't spotted anyone they knew, there were more pictures showing up on Tenacity socials.

Vicky was enjoying putting on a show and Archer was a dedicated partner who was taking his job very seriously. Something interesting was happening, something that made her feel as if they were the real deal, not a couple who had just pulled off a convenient marriage. She was becoming used to holding on to Archer and she had an inkling he felt the same. The more they hugged and kissed and flirted, the more she wanted to do those things. It had become rather natural to feel his biceps, put her hand on his thigh, run her fingers across his gorgeous pecs. He was a really handsome man, and it certainly wasn't a chore to touch him. And, boy, did his lips pack a punch when they kissed. She had begun to imagine what it would feel like to have this strong rancher's hands on her naked skin.

"Heaven."

"Come again?" Archer asked.

Had she said that aloud? Praying her blush wouldn't betray her real meaning, she leaned into a PDA and snuggled up to him. "I meant this is heaven. Being here with you. I hate to leave."

Ignoring everyone sitting at the bar, he focused on her. "Yeah. I get it," he said. "But we've got to get back. Work on the ranch is building up."

She nodded. "It's hard for May Bell to run the shop on her own. We don't discuss it. It's an unspoken agreement that when I see her struggling, I just step up. I open the shop, or I close the shop. She counts on me. And now that my community service is done, I need to get the store caught up, too." Then she added, "But I will miss this."

He leaned over, snuck a quick kiss in before he stood and held out his hand. "I guess we need to start packing up."

Holding hands, they walked slowly to the elevators as if they were trying to slow down time.

"I think we've taken a hold of the narrative about our relationship," she said. "Don't you?"

He nodded his agreement.

"I like being on your arm," she told him, her guard down. "I'm proud to be on your arm."

He brought her hand up and kissed it. "I'm grateful for that."

Once in their room, they packed up in short order and then sat out on the balcony. It had become a quiet time that they both enjoyed. There were long silences between them, but it didn't feel awkward to either of them. Archer had maintained she rest and put up her feet while they enjoyed their time outside. He'd become insistent that she take care of herself during her pregnancy. His concern was meaningful to her. And, when their marriage ended, she already knew that she would miss his support.

It's just you and me, kid. People will come and go, but you will always have me.

"Room service?" His question broke into her thoughts.

The food arrived and they sat together for dinner, and Archer brought up logistics of their marriage.

"We need to get you moved into my cabin," her husband said. "I can help pack up your apartment. I know Graham and Cassie would pitch in, too."

"Well," she said, after wiping her mouth with the cloth napkin, "I'm still going to maintain my apartment. I love it and one day, down the road, when we decide that this deal between us needs to end, it'll be my home again."

Archer's expression was difficult to read, and he took some time to respond. "That makes sense."

Despite his words, Vicky wasn't so convinced that Archer

felt it was a good idea. If they intended to make the town believe that their marriage was real and the baby she carried was his, why would she keep an apartment?

"If anyone asks, we can just say that I'm halfway on my lease," she reasoned. "Doesn't make financial sense to lose that money."

Archer nodded, dropped his napkin on his plate and then stood up from the table. She was sensing that she had completely torpedoed the good mood of the evening. He rolled the cart into the hallway, then turned to her. "I'm thinking of hitting the hay early."

"Me, too," she said, disappointed. They had planned to explore each other's playlists or rent a horror movie.

Archer headed to the bathroom he had been using, and she retreated to her own bathroom to get one last soak in that tub.

While she was soaking and rubbing her hands over her belly, she tried to retrace the conversation they'd had over dinner to figure out what had gone wrong.

She got out of the tub carefully, began to drain the water, and dried off with the hotel towel that was large enough to wrap around her belly twice. She hadn't planned on being pregnant at this time in her life, but she was all-in and excited to be a mom, something she had dreamed about since she was a kid. However, that didn't mean that every part of pregnancy was zen and bliss. She hadn't put on much weight beyond what her doctor in Bronco had suggested. She hadn't fallen into that tempting "I'm eating for two" mindset. But looking at her naked body now, she loved her belly, and yes, her breasts were larger, and she could fill out a top like no other time in her life. At times, she didn't feel beautiful. At times, she felt like she couldn't carry one more pound of weight comfortably. And then she thought of her baby, Riley. That was when she could rise above her self-criticism and embrace this moment and this body.

Once she was comfy in her nighty, robe, and slippers, she

pulled her hair up in a ponytail, then began her new bedtime routine. She massaged in the face creams she'd been gifted when having the facial Archer had set up for her as a surprise. She brushed her teeth and opened the bathroom door, expecting to see Archer on his side of the bed, either scrolling through his phone or on his way to sleep. But she didn't find him in bed. Curious, she walked out to the living room and found that Archer had made a makeshift bed on the couch. The immediate feeling she had was hurt. Rejection and hurt. What had she done or said that was so bad that, on the last night of their honeymoon, he would rather sleep on the couch instead of in the bed with her?

"Archer?" She had thought to turn around and let it be. But then, she just couldn't.

Archer opened his eyes.

"Why aren't you in bed?"

"I'm going to catch some shut-eye here."

She looked at him—his eyes closed again, basically giving her the brush-off—and decided that just wasn't going to work for her.

"Please sit up and tell me what the heck is going on. Give me that respect."

That turn of phrase did what she had wanted. He bolted up like a shot, threw the spare comforter off his legs and stood.

"I'm out here *because* I respect you!"

"Archer, I don't under—"

He cut her off. "I can't sleep in that bed with you, Vicky. Okay? Let's just leave it at that."

"No." She rested her hands on her hips. "I'm not going to be able to sleep if you don't tell me what's wrong!"

"I can't sleep in there with you, Vicky."

"Why?" she asked. Once. Twice.

"Goddamn it!" Archer cursed. "I *crowd* you."

Vicky shook her head while her brain tried to piece together a picture of him *crowding* her in bed and came up empty.

"Archer, what are you talking about?"

Archer blew out a breath, ran his hands over his head several times, while he examined the floor.

"I start out on one side of the bed." He waved his hand in defeat, she supposed. "When I wake up, I'm on your side of the bed."

More processing. What was this about? Spooning? Cuddling?

"You're not bothering me," she told him. "You aren't being disrespectful."

Silence followed with Archer still running his hand over his head before he looked her dead in the eye.

"Okay. I'm going to give you the unvarnished truth."

"Good."

"Let the chips fall where they may."

"Okay."

He gestured with his hand like he was cutting the air. "I'm attracted to you."

"Why is that a problem?"

"Vicky—" He restarted. "When we're in bed together, sometimes—" He stopped. "No. Correction, all of the time, I think about—"

"Sex."

"Well, I was going to say making love."

"Okay. But when we're in bed together, did it ever occur to you that I might think about sex, too?"

Now Archer's curiosity was piqued. "Is that right?"

"Yes, Archer!" She lifted her hands, palms up. "Fun fact, some women have an elevated libido during pregnancy, and I happen to be, as I have discovered, a woman who falls in that particular category."

"So, you've thought about it."

"Yes. Often."

"Every night?"

"Every night, every morning," she confessed. "All that hugging and kissing we've been doing in order to sell our marriage as real… Well, I'm only human."

"So am I," Archer said. Her husband had deliberately allowed her to see a sensual glint in his eyes accompanied by a sensual undertone in his voice.

The way he was looking at her now that she had confessed to having carnal thoughts about him made the room feel charged with electricity. She could feel the tension between them in every part of her body.

He took a step toward her, and he let her see in his eyes, for the first time, the desire he had for her. It was animalistic, and she felt her body responding. He wanted her; she wanted him.

"I didn't bring you to Thunder Canyon for that," he told her. "I hope you know that."

"I do," she said emphatically.

"We can figure it out." They each took a step toward the other. "If you're open to it."

"I'm open to it," she said. "Of course, we haven't fully explored the ramifications of us consummating the marriage or the 'friends with benefits' kind of a deal, because we entered into this union as platonic friends."

"Things change."

"Yes. They often do."

"And we are married." He held up his left hand to show the band of gold he wore.

"That's true." She held up her ring finger. "We are married. If we want to make love, it isn't anyone's business."

"Except for Cassie," he added.

"Except for Cassie."

"And Graham, because she'll tell him."

"True."

They had closed the distance between them and now stood

only inches apart. "I've never made love with a woman who is pregnant. I was worried. About hurting Riley. So, I asked Siri."

That caught her off guard and made her laugh, and then he started to laugh with her and the tension crackling in the air was washed away.

"And what did Siri AI say?" she asked him.

"Baby will be okay."

"Archer?" She took his hands in hers. "Do you want to make love to me?"

"Yes." Simple. No frills. Just straight to the point. "If you want me to."

"I do."

Archer got the green light, and he was finished with the talking. He threaded his fingers together behind her hair, tilting her face gently up, and then he kissed her. Long, deep, full of the pent-up passion of a man who had been tortured with wanting her. It was the best, most honest kiss of her life. His arms drew her closer as he dropped sensuous kisses down her neck and along her collar bone.

"If I had known that this was going happen, I would have picked different underwear," she managed to say. "These are just 'granny panties' with belly support."

"I don't care." He guided her to the bed. "They're coming off anyway."

Archer was quick to strip off his clothes, but he was slow and thoughtful with her comfy nighty and full-coverage panties. It was amazing how his rough, callused hands could be so gentle.

"I love the way you smell," he whispered.

"Hmm. Me, too you."

Just as they often slept, Archer had wrapped his body around hers, his hand on her belly, his lips kissing the back of her neck, sending lovely chills up and down her spine. Bells, whistles, fireworks going off, toes curling, heart racing, moans and shallow breathing. She felt everything all at once. This was new.

This was different. Never in her wildest dreams could her body feel this way, and the cowboy really hadn't even gotten started.

His breath on her ear, he whispered, "Mrs. Callahan, would you like me to make love to you?"

"Mr. Callahan, isn't there something better for your lips to be doing other than talking?"

He nibbled on her ear and said, "Mrs. Callahan, you're about to find out."

Archer was fast asleep in the bed and she, unable to sleep, went out to the balcony.

Now alone with her thoughts, she realized opening the sexual door with Archer was going to complicate things. She had never been a "friends with benefits" kind of girl. Archer was only her third lover. Yet, they were husband and wife. For now. Should she let her feelings lead on occasion?

She put her phone in her robe pocket, walked over to the balcony railing and looked up at the stars, so bright this evening. Archer had inspired a new interest in the stars and the universe. Now she looked at the stars with a newfound curiosity. After several moments more out on the balcony she had so enjoyed, Vicky went back inside and headed to bed.

In the dark, Archer asked, "Everything okay?"

"Yes."

He lifted the covers for her. "Coming back to bed?"

"Yes."

She got herself into bed, put a pillow between her knees and rested her head on Archer's arm. As she snuggled into him, enjoying the warmth of his body and the feeling of his hand on her belly, Vicky pushed aside her constant worrying about the future and simply enjoyed the moment. Had they just made their complicated relationship more complicated? One hundred percent.

Chapter Twelve

The next morning, they grabbed a quick breakfast, checked out of the resort, and got on the road just in time to see a spectacular sunrise.

"Back to reality," Archer said.

It was bittersweet for her as well. She had loved spending time at the resort with Archer, getting to know him, and she felt much more connected to her husband, and not just because they had made love. At the moment, they had an early morning mission to head back to Tenacity, so there hadn't been time to see if their decision to cross that line made things awkward between them. When sex was put into the mix, it usually had an effect, not always positive.

"Let's make a plan," Archer said. "What do we need to get done right off the bat?"

"Besides our day jobs," she said. She pulled up an app on her phone so she could generate a list and share that list with Archer. "I need to pack up what I'm going to move to your place."

"Yep." He nodded. "Once you're all packed up, I'll get Graham to help me with loading up your stuff and move you in."

He said it so matter-of-factly but, inside, Vicky was nervous about the move in general. The cabin was nice. For somebody else. The privacy was wonderful. For somebody else. Unending views of pastureland with grazing cattle was tranquil. For somebody else. Other than her family, she hadn't lived with anyone in her life. Yes, her apartment was tiny, but it was hers. Every inch of it, hers. The two of them managed to get a preview of living together in the honeymoon suite, but a vacation setting was far from real life. The bills, the chores, work schedules, family, all had an impact. Then you throw a baby into the mix and this could very well be a recipe for disaster.

They continued making their to-do list and Vicky was grateful for the distraction. Archer didn't seem to be living in regret for the extracurricular activity they had participated in their last night in the honeymoon suite. On her end, she was on the fence. She didn't want to regret it; she wanted to make their marriage of convenience work until it could be terminated. What wouldn't be so easy to discard? The hormone, oxytocin, also called the love hormone, the one that helps mothers bond with their babies, was released during lovemaking. That meant, whether it was a good idea or not to sleep with Archer, her brain and body now saw him as a wonderful place to go for the trifecta of happy hormones.

"Anything else?" Archer asked.

"No." She shook her head. "Oh. Other than I see my new OBGYN this week."

"Okay. Let me know day and time so I can be there."

That made her go quiet. When she'd first realized she was pregnant by her estranged boyfriend, and Louis didn't want to be a part of his baby's life, Vicky had begun to think of Riley as hers and hers alone. There were many examples of women who were strong, resourceful single moms. Of course, it was important for Riley to have strong male role models, but she didn't need a husband for that. She had Brent, and Graham, and even Archer if they could dissolve their marriage amicably as planned.

"Vicky?"

"Oh. Sorry. My mind drifted," she said. "You know, you don't have to come to the appointment. I'm used to going it alone."

Now Archer seemed caught off guard. "You have me now. You don't have to go it alone."

How could she argue with that?

"I know," Vicky said. "But you just have so much to catch up on at the ranch."

Archer glanced over at her, his brows drawn. After some silence between them, he asked, "Is there a reason you don't want me to be there?"

Darn it.

"No. Not really. No," she said. "I just feel, I guess, protective."

His expression let her know that she hadn't made anything clearer.

"When I found out I was pregnant, while I was still dealing with the fallout from the scandal, I only had myself. And Cassie. But there was only so much she could do."

Archer seemed to take the information in, mull it over, and then said, "I understand your reasoning. When you're used to doing everything alone, not by choice, but by necessity, you have to be independent. The idea of leaning on someone, for even a small thing, could feel like removing bricks, one by one, until your wall falls down."

Now, Vicky was caught off guard. She hadn't known Archer for long, but for him to summarize and interpret what she felt inside yet hadn't been able to fully articulate amazed her. He was a man who felt things deeply, despite his rugged, macho exterior.

"Yes, that's right," Vicky said softly.

"The way I was thinking about it was from the angle of always showing Tenacity happy newlyweds and expectant parents. If I was the father, I'd be there."

She couldn't deny that Archer had a valid point. Now that they were back home, every move they made had to be convincing. Natural. Easy. Undeniable. Before, she'd felt her OBGYN appointments were special, and she didn't want anything regarding her child sullied by the need she felt to deceive Tenacity, even if that deception was to protect Riley from any negative fallout from her family's past transgressions. But now she realized Archer was right.

"I think you should come," she told him.

Archer glanced at her as he took the exit to Tenacity.

"But only if you want to come," she added.

"I want to come, Vicky. And not just because of optics. Okay? I care about you and I care about Riley."

"Thank you."

They hit the first red light heading into town.

"We're home," she said with a notable wariness in her voice.

"Yep."

Then Archer asked, "Are you going to find out Riley's gender at this appointment?"

"No. The gender was determined during my first trimester."

"You know?"

"No. I want the gender to be a surprise," she explained. "Anyway, I couldn't have a gender-reveal party or a baby shower for a baby only Louis and Cassie knew about. I did have my doctor write the gender down and put it an envelope. I gave it to Cassie so I wouldn't be tempted to peek and ruin the surprise."

"But if you hadn't had to hide it, would you have this gender reveal deal Cassie's always talking about?"

She shrugged. "I'm sure I would have. I had to accept reality or go nuts. So I just decided to wait until Riley came and that would the best gender reveal of all gender reveals!"

In what seemed like a blink of an eye, Archer had parked in front of her apartment. Once they were inside, she immediately took note of her plants and provided emergency water to some and light to others.

"I should have asked Cassie to water them."

"They look like they'll live."

She smiled. Archer could always make her smile. "I'd like to bring them, if that's okay."

"We accept all manner of plants at the ranch." He walked to the door. "I'm going to head out. You okay for now?"

"Yes," she said. "I'll get some boxes from the grocery. Mrs. Chen always has empty boxes around. I'll do her a favor and take some off her hands."

"I'm going to assess things at the ranch and then I'll come back this evening to load you up."

"Sounds good."

At the door, Archer turned back to her. "How about a good-bye kiss?" he said.

"There isn't anybody watching us."

"I think we should keep up the practice."

With a faint smile, she lifted onto her tiptoes and kissed him.

"See you later, darlin'," her husband said with a tip of the brim of his hat.

She shut the door and then leaned back against it, hands resting, as they usually did, on her rounded belly.

"This is really happening, Riley. Ready or not, Callahan family, here we come."

"Hey, brother!" Archer found Graham and Cooper in one of the horse pastures fixing the automatic waterer.

"We missed you, man." Graham greeted him with a smile, handshake, and hug. Next, Archer greeted Cooper affectionately. Graham pulled off his hat, ran his shirtsleeve over his forehead to wipe off some of the sweat before he turned back to the job.

"Need a hand?" Archer asked.

"I always need a hand," his eldest brother said.

"Funny how you turned up right when the job was almost over." Cooper smiled.

Together they took the outside casing off the waterer and

then began to go through each component. They replaced some small parts that had rusted away. The work was quiet, as usual. After they put the waterer back in place and then tested the mechanisms, it was gratifying to see fresh water coming into the basin. The horses had spotted the brothers, and they galloped toward them. All of the horses in this pasture were older, retired from ranch work, but for Archer, they were at their best.

"Hi, there, big fella." He rubbed the forehead of a thirty-year-old Appaloosa with a red body and brown, red, and white dapples on the rump.

With all of the horses vying for the fresh water, Archer and his two brothers gave some love to each of the horses before they headed back to the trucks they had left parked on the other side of the pasture gate. When he was younger, and after they lost their father in a tragic accident with a horse, Archer had been wary around horses for several years. But his brothers knew that in order for him to inherit his part of their birthright, to work the land and to live the life of a rancher, he had to overcome his fear. With the strong, steady hands of his brothers, he did overcome that fear.

Graham offered him a drink from the cooler. He accepted. Now leaning against the front end of Cooper's truck, Archer gulped down the cold water while he waited for the questions he was certain that his brothers had at the forefront of their minds.

"Cassie tells me you had a good time at the resort," Graham said.

"We did," Archer said. "That's for sure."

Then Graham jumped over all the small talk and said, "No matter how hard I try, I just can't get it through my thick head the why behind this marriage, Archer. Why in the world did you tie yourself down with this woman?"

Archer bristled. "Do you mean my wife?"

"Your wife for *now*, Arch. For *now*."

Archer threw his empty bottle into the back of his truck to

be thrown away later. "All any of us have is right now," Archer replied to Graham.

Graham shook his head as he tossed up his hands in frustration. "Don't go getting all philosophical on me, brother. I'm just looking out for you."

Cooper was looking frustrated with both of them. "Graham, you're wrong man. Just wrong. We had this talk and it was settled. The marriage is done. They're married. Move on. We've got too many irons in the fire to be fighting each other."

"I hear you, Cooper, but Graham needs to hear this," Archer said through gritted teeth. He didn't need to be taking on friendly fire his first day back. "When you cooked up the scheme to have Cassie pose as your girlfriend during your campaign, I supported you."

"True," Cooper said. "He did."

"I didn't agree with it, but I supported you. *And* I voted for you."

"Thank you for your vote," Graham said with a small smirk. He was the kind of man who could see his wrong pretty quick and do his best to set it right. "And I do get what you're saying."

"I need you to have my back on this one." Archer leaned back again, arms crossed in front of his chest. "Both of you, and Ash, too. I've got real feelings for Vicky. I mean real feelings. It's not like before. I was just a kid then. I'm not a kid anymore."

"But you'll always be our baby brother." Graham sighed. "Does she have feelings for you?"

"Damned if I know." Archer shook his head. "Vicky's always been a bag of mixed messages. But I would never walk away from this until I know if there is something deeper between us."

"I hope you come out of this thing in one piece."

"You and me both." Archer was done talking about his relationship with Vicky. "What's next on today's to-do list?"

"Harvesting hay in the north and west pastures." Cooper filled him in. "If you two could take the lead on that, I'll take the trailer to Tenacity Feed and Seed to pick up some supplies. Running low on feed across the board."

Archer gave him a thumb's-up, heading to his truck before he remembered something. "Hey!"

Graham had his arm resting on the open window of his truck, engine already running and ready to go. Cooper was heading to the driver's side of his truck.

"Yeah?" his brothers asked in near unison.

"I need you to help me move Vicky into my place later."

"We almost got a clean getaway, didn't we?" Graham said to Cooper with good humor.

"Darn close." Archer waved his hand. "I'll text you guys with a time later."

And with that, they all parted ways, to divide and conquer ranch chores. That's what Archer loved about ranch life. It was different every day. Always something new to do, something to fix, new animals to integrate. He was a Montana rancher to his core; it was a part of his DNA. Could Vicky ever truly adapt to this life? With so much working against them already, if Vicky couldn't learn to love the ranch, there weren't feelings deep enough to hold them together. Fake marriage. Real marriage. Marriage of convenience. Any marriage to him would be grounded in ranch life. Vicky was moving in today; time would tell if she could learn to love this land the way he did. If she truly loved him, she would find a way.

Vicky had been busy packing everything she thought she would need while she lived in Archer's cabin. Mrs. Chen was happy to give her as many boxes as she needed with an open invitation for more. Vicky did notice something rather strange while she was in the grocery store. People were being friendlier, smiling at her, saying hello instead of giving her the angry side-eye or looking at her with the same pity they would give to an abandoned puppy. Some even congratulated her on her recent nuptials.

"It's bizarre," she told Cassie. "But I hope it continues. I felt like a normal person."

"You're a married woman now with a baby on the way. Everyone loves babies."

Redemption. That was the word that came to mind. Had she turned a corner in this town? Oh, how she hoped she had. Not so much for her sake, but for Riley's.

"Topic shift." Vicky folded some of her new maternity jeans and tops and put them in a produce box. "Archer is coming with me for my first OBGYN appointment."

"Well, that screams *commitment.*"

"I don't know about that." Vicky's eyebrows lowered in thought. "But I believe him when he says he cares about me and my baby."

"There is no way Archer would go through all of this if he didn't have feelings for you."

"I know he has feelings for me, Cass. I have feelings for him. We were—are—friends," Vicky said. "Then we started leaning into PDA to convince Tenacity that we are in love."

"I have seen the pics." Cassie laughed. "*Get a room* was the most frequent comment."

"I saw that," Vicky said. "All of that kissing and hugging and flirting. That made us bond in a way neither one of us expected. But long-term? I just can't focus on that when I need to get ready for Riley."

"Are you still determined to be surprised by the gender? I can tell you if you are having a Riley Cassandra or a Riley Brent."

"Archer just asked me about that."

"I know the answer." Cassie teased in a singsong voice.

"Well, just keep on keeping it to yourself! I still want to be surprised."

* * *

The first night in Archer's cabin was uncomfortable. Boxes were stacked up in the living room, the refrigerator only had condiments, a case of beer, butter, and a head of lettuce that had seen better days.

"How's it going?" Archer checked on her.

"Just getting the lay of the land," she said, still feeling annoyed that Archer wouldn't budge on the room arrangement.

"We'll get some groceries in here tomorrow," he promised.

"Okay," she said. "Right now, I just need to find a spoon."

Archer smiled at her. "Mint-chocolate-chip."

Cassie had come along with Graham to help her move—and, of course, along with takeout for all of them, her bestie knew that it wouldn't be home without mint-chocolate-chip in the freezer.

Archer headed off to the spare bathroom to get cleaned up. After he'd moved her in, Graham and he had to head out to round up some cattle that had broken through one of the gates.

By the time he had come home, it was well past dark, his clothes were dirty and sweaty, his boots were dusty, there were smudges on his face, and he smelled like he'd been in a fight with a cow and lost. When she asked him how often he was called to action on the ranch at night, he told her, "The ranch never sleeps."

Tenacity wasn't a big town, but the street that her apartment overlooked got busy at peak times and that noise had become a part of her life. The noises coming from around Archer's woodland cabin? Those noises were creepy. Rustling, whistling wind, unknown things landing on the tin roof, an odd hooting sound that she figured was an owl doing what owls do at night. The light on the porch was activated by motion and that darn thing kept going off and on. She loved Brent's ranch but she hadn't stayed there at night. This was a new experience entirely and she was pretty sure that she didn't like it. Bright side? Even though Cassie hadn't officially moved in with Graham, she spent a good deal of time at the ranch.

"You found a spoon." Having just showered, Archer now wore clean jeans, a button-down shirt unbuttoned, and his dark blond hair slicked back from his handsome face. All she could think was, *I married one sexy man.*

And that thought sent her mind spiraling off to an instant replay of their lovemaking the night before. So good. So very good. Sensual, gentle, and satisfying. Mind right into the gutter.

Archer got a glass of water and then nodded toward the stack of still-wrapped wedding gifts. "What should we do with those?"

Vicky rolled her eyes and sighed. They had asked everyone not to bring a gift and, because of the bounty before them, it appeared that there wasn't a guest who had done as requested.

"I don't know," she said. "I think we need to open them, write a thank-you note, put them aside and give them back later?"

Archer thought about it and agreed. "Makes sense."

"Let's open them tomorrow so I can write the notes."

"Sounds good," Archer said. "You look tuckered."

She yawned loudly. "You, too."

"Let's hit the sack. I've got an early morning, and don't you open Nothin' New?"

"Yes."

Archer turned off the lights in the living room and kitchen and followed her down the hallway. She kept on to the main bedroom only to realize that she had lost Archer along the way. She turned around and saw him going into the spare room.

"Archer?"

He turned to her.

"Why are you sleeping in there?" she asked, puzzled.

Now he looked puzzled. "That was our arrangement."

"Before the honeymoon," she pointed out. "We've been

sleeping in the same bed since our wedding day. You can sleep in here with me."

"I didn't want to assume."

"I get that." He was a rancher and a gentleman. "But this is us now."

"Are you sure?"

"Positive." She waved her hand. "Come on. You need your rest, and that spare bed? I swear every spring in that torture device has sprung. I wouldn't wish that on my worst enemy."

While they were getting into the bed together, what Vicky held back about offering to share his bed was the fact that over the short time on the honeymoon, she had grown to love the feel of his weight in the bed. She had grown to find comfort in his arm holding her when he eventually rolled over to her side. Vicky wanted them both to be comfortable, and the best way for that to be achieved was for them to continue sharing a bed.

While this new arrangement felt scary, it also felt exciting. How could she have known that sleeping in the same bed with her husband could set off some very naughty thoughts. Perhaps that was a reason to keep things as is. Why was everything so complicated and convoluted? Would her life ever just be straightforward?

"Good night, Vic."

"Good night."

Archer was certainly tired, but he couldn't manage to fall asleep. He lay on his back, right arm behind his head. When he'd put all of this in motion by asking Vicky out on a date, he hadn't anticipated marrying the lovely Miss Woodson and moving her into his home. Yet, that's what had happened. He had wanted to get to know her, yes. Things had spun out of control. He had begun to know her, and he had begun to believe that she was his person. And he had also begun to get attached to her and attached to her child in a way that left him feeling vulnerable.

Vicky stirred, turned her body to face him, and like a heat-seeking missile, she found her way to his side of the bed, curled her body closer to him, her belly pressed into his side, her head on his arm, her hand on his chest. The sweet scent of honeysuckle in her thick hair, the softness of her skin, made him aware of the roughness of his own hands; and the memories of their lovemaking made him need to turn away from his wife and roll out of bed. That drew an unhappy noise from Vicky, but he went anyway, to lie down on the couch so he could get his mind straight. He must have dozed off, because he awakened to the sound of water running in the main bathroom, and then Vicky's footsteps coming out to the living room.

"Archer?"

"I'm right here on the couch, Vic." He sat up. It was still night and the room was dark.

"Oh." He could hear the disappointment in her voice. "Why?"

Archer stood up. "I get hot sometimes. I must have dozed off. I'm coming."

Archer followed his wife back to bed and something happened for the first time in his life. Hearing the hurt in his wife's voice felt like a knife to the gut. Her hurt felt worse than his own.

Archer slid under the sheets and then slid his body over to Vicky, who was facing away from him. He put his arm around her, and she didn't resist, so he kissed her bare shoulder and told her good-night with a silent promise to himself that he was going to work overtime to stop hurting Vicky. No matter what happened to their relationship in the future, Vicky had already endured so much…he didn't need to pile on.

Chapter Thirteen

By the time she had her appointment with her new doctor in Tenacity, Vicky was actually feeling settled in at the cabin. She'd found the perfect spot for her plants, and she'd unpacked her things. Archer really didn't have much by the way of clothing—mainly boots, hats, jeans, button-down shirts. So, there was good space for her to feel at home. She had also found an abandoned greenhouse hidden behind some overgrown foliage near the cabin. Archer used a chainsaw and hatchet to let her get a better look and, as it turned out, the little building was on life support but could be given new life with some elbow grease and love. That was a project she thought would keep her mind busy when she was feeling out of place on the ranch.

On the other side of her brain was the part that overthought every single look, word, gesture, or lack thereof, from Archer. She had noticed that he was leaving his wedding ring off when he went to work on the ranch. Ever since the age of twelve when she had hidden that money, she'd developed a high-alert part of her personality, always looking for evidence that her secret had been found out. Now that her secret was out and she was moving on with her life, she noticed that the high-alert part of her brain hadn't gotten the memo to stand down. Instead, now she just overanalyzed her relationship with Archer. It was exhausting. Every night, they both fell into bed after a quick dinner, too tired to do much else. Or was Archer deliberately shutting her out and turning her off?

On her way to the doctor's office, Vicky shopped the sale area of Tenacity Feed and Seed for potting plants, seeds, and fertilizer.

"Looks like you're starting a project," the cashier said.

"I am," Vicky said with a genuine smile. "Fixing up a greenhouse."

"Wonderful."

"That's not bad at all," she said, putting her bank card into the point of sale. "I love a bargain."

The cashier handed her the receipt, and she was off with her gardening supplies. She opened the back of her SUV and bemoaned the lack of storage. Living on the ranch for a short time had changed her perspective. She needed more boots, less sandals. She needed more jeans, less flowy dresses. And she needed a truck bed to store all of her items that didn't really go inside a vehicle. When she told Archer what she wanted to do, he was going to smile at her with that glint in his eye. She looked forward to it.

"Why is this so low to the ground?" Vicky complained about her compact SUV. It used to be the perfect vehicle for her but now with her belly, as well as her newfound appreciation for riding up high in Archer's truck, she was less than thrilled. She had to move the seat almost all the way back, but she made it work.

"Okay, Riley," she said. "Let's get you checked out."

Vicky found a space in the parking lot and then headed inside. On the way, she spotted Archer's truck. Once again he'd kept his word to her, and was, as always, ever punctual. She found him in the waiting room.

"Hey." He greeted her with a quick kiss.

"Hi."

She had already filled out the paperwork and given them her identification, which allowed her to get herself checked in quickly and join Archer on a sofa.

Archer reached for her hand, and she was grateful for the

support. Of course, she believed that things were fine with Riley—she watched her diet, took suggested vitamins, didn't drink caffeine, and she attended all of her checkups and did her best, as much as her life would allow, to keep her stress levels down.

"Thank you for coming."

He squeezed her hand in response.

When Archer had wanted to attend the appointment, her immediate response was to push him away. It was a defense mechanism, she believed. So many people in her life had let her down, it was difficult to trust. It was even harder for her to lean on anyone. She had to be strong.

"Did you find anything for the nursery?" He leaned over to ask.

She took out her phone and scrolled through what she had found in her online searches.

"Looks good. I like it," Archer said, looking at a picture of a crib. "If you need me to help you put that together, I'm your man."

He was her man in more ways than one. In such a short time he had become very important to her. For a long time, her circle of trust was three deep: Brent, Cassie, and May Bell. Now, though, she found Archer deserving of her trust. Thanks to him, when she pondered what she would tell Riley if her child discovered that her family was built on lies, Vicky was learning how to forgive her twelve-year-old self. She had punished herself enough.

"Vicky Woodson?"

Vicky stood up and Archer followed suit. They were led to a room after she weighed in.

"Wow," she said of her weight. "Riley is going to be a big baby."

"Is that the name you've picked out?" the nurse asked.

"Yes. Good for a girl or a boy."

"I love that," the nurse said. "We'll collect a quick urine sample and then you can join us in room two."

Vicky gave her sample and headed to room two, where the nurse took her vitals.

After the nurse recorded the vitals, she then told them that the ultrasound technician would be in to see them in a moment.

Archer was looking out of place sitting in a chair next to a 3-D model of the female genitalia and any part of the body involved in pregnancy. He took his hat off and put it over the model. To the right of his chair, there was a rather aggressively large-framed, colored and labeled poster of the same anatomy. Archer stared at it for a bit before he pushed himself upright and turned slightly to the left.

"Doing okay over there, cowboy?"

Archer said, "Livin' the dream."

That made her laugh, and he cracked a smile.

"Why don't you come sit in the chair next to me," she said. "There isn't a giant poster of a vagina."

Archer flushed bright red and took her advice.

Next to her, he'd be able to see the ultrasound. She realized she actually wanted him to see Riley. This was a seismic shift in her thinking. This was the first appointment that she didn't want to just be Riley and her. But she didn't have time to analyze that shift as the technician came in.

"We will be looking at your baby's anatomy using the ultrasound. We will check organs, heart, brain, spine, kidneys, and limbs. I will also take measurements to see if your baby is growing at a proper rate. The scan will also let me check the amniotic fluid and position of the placenta."

The technician reclined the examination table while Vicky lifted up her shirt and opened her jeans. A little bit of gel on the skin to help the wand move over her belly and then Riley popped up on the screen.

"There's your baby and your baby's heartbeat."

She glanced over at Archer, and his eyes were trained on the screen, laser focused.

Not even trying to play it cool, he said, "Wow. That's Riley?"

"It is," she told her husband.

"Do you know the gender?" the technician asked. "Do you want to know?"

"No," Vicky said less quickly than before, she realized. "I want it to be a surprise."

"Gender reveal party?" the technician asked with a smile.

"I'm considering it."

The ultrasound concluded and the technician told them that Dr. Parker would be in shortly.

When they were alone in the room, Archer still seemed stunned. For the second time, she asked, "Are you okay?"

Archer shook his head. "I wasn't expecting to be able to see Riley. Like that."

Archer didn't seem focused on her physical being in a bad way. Instead, all of his focus was on Riley. Darn her mixed emotions! Part of her wanted some of the attention on her, but she couldn't be upset by Archer's interest in her baby.

She was back to sitting up, her clothing in place. A knock on the door, and a middle-aged woman entered. She was slender, with her hair clipped at the nape of her neck.

"Hi, I'm Dr. Parker," she said. "Vicky Woodson?"

"Yes." Vicky nodded. "And this is my husband, Archer."

In the waiting room, Vicky had read a pamphlet introducing Dr. Parker. She was a Montana native who had returned to her home state to start her practice. She had picked Tenacity because it reminded her of her childhood visits to Tenacity Trail. The doctor shook Archer's hand and then hers. "It's nice to meet both of you. I've reviewed your records from Bronco."

The doctor laid her back again and conducted a quick physical exam of her own before helping her upright. "Well, it's all great news. Growth is on track, all organs are developing as expected—brain, heart, lungs all look spot on. There aren't any signs of diabetes, your weight is good. Maybe add some gentle exercise. Walking or swimming."

"That's great news," Archer said.

Dr. Parker smiled at him. "Excited father-to-be."

Then Dr. Parker asked them both, "Do you have any questions for me?"

"No," Vicky said. "Thank you for taking me on."

"My pleasure. Let me know if you have any questions or concerns." Dr. Parker stood, shook their hands, and then directed them to reception to set up the next appointment.

Outside, Archer saw Vicky to her car. He asked, "Are you heading back to the ranch?"

She nodded. "You?"

"No. I've got to head over to the auction."

He opened the door for her, shut it when she was behind the wheel, then gestured for her to roll down the window. She knew that he wanted to give her a kiss. Archer was always aware of the need to sell the "real newlyweds" image to the townsfolk of Tenacity.

"I'll see you tonight," Vicky said with a wave and then rolled the window back up and put the vehicle in Reverse.

Archer followed her, tapped on the window with his knuckle.

Back down went the window.

"Vic," he said, his striking green eyes sincere, "thank you for letting me come."

"Of course. Thank you for coming."

"I'll never forget it," he said. "Seeing Riley for the first time. I'll never forget it."

Archer came home after a long day of selling and buying used equipment at the auction. They were always changing out old equipment and finding deals on tractors, trailers, and balers to cut up the hayfields. Archer used one of the ranch's heavy-duty trucks to haul the equipment for sale and to bring back his purchases. His clothing was covered in dirt and oil and several layers of sweat, and all he wanted to do was strip down, take a long shower, and spend some time with Vicky. That incredible experience at the doctor's appointment had been at the forefront of his mind. He couldn't shake the image of Riley moving, heart beating. Nothing had prepared him for how he felt seeing those images of Riley.

Archer sat down on the top step of the porch and yanked off his boots. Vicky had been keeping a clean house, and he didn't want to track the auction into the cabin. Vicky called it "decorating with feng shui, allowing the flow of energy." He didn't know much about it other than his wife got mad as all get-out when he tracked mud, dirt, or manure into the house.

"Vic?" he called out to her. "Hey, Vic," he called out again. "Are you in here?"

When he couldn't find Vicky, he went outside, put his boots back on to go to the greenhouse. The only places she went were inside the cabin and the greenhouse. That was as adventurous as she had been with exploration of the ranch.

"Hey, there." He found Vicky in the greenhouse.

"Oh, hi!"

"What're you up to?"

Vicky's face was glowing with happiness and excitement. He had always thought Vicky was cute and sassy in a girl-next-door kind of way. But in this light, in the place where she could take care of her plants, doing what she loved, Vicky was stunning. And she quite literally took his breath away.

"Look!" she said. "I shopped the sale room at Tenacity Feed and Seed. I am going to grow tomatoes, basil, zucchini, carrots, and cucumbers. What do you think?"

"I think it's great," he said honestly. "Looking forward to eating what you grow."

"Me, too!"

Any sign, no matter how tiny and seemingly insignificant, that Vicky might be able to adapt to ranch life gave him a glimmer of hope. He knew it was tough going for her. There were bugs and flying insects one did not encounter in town. Depending on the wind, the scent of cow manure was unavoidable.

"Did you see the boxes?" she asked as she put away her supplies.

"I did. I'll crack those open after I shower."

Vicky followed him out but took one last look at her progress in the greenhouse before she closed the door behind them.

"I do need water out there," she said.

"I'll get that fixed for you," he told her.

He slowed his pace so they could walk side by side. He stopped just before the first step to the porch. "Ladies first."

Vicky started up the stairs but then seemed to teeter to the right. He reached for her hand, helped steady her, and while his heart was beating hard with concern, she laughed self-effacingly.

He was too wary to joke around. Vicky could injure herself at any time: today, he was here. Would he be here the next time?

They both took off their footwear before going inside.

"I just threw together a salad and made some subs," she said to him. "Hope that works for you."

"More than okay." He headed off to the shower.

Before Vicky, he'd grab a can of beans and a beer and call it dinner. She was spoiling him, and he couldn't deny that he liked it a whole lot.

Archer emerged from the bathroom and nodded to the wet ball of clothing from the day in his arms. "Where do I put these?"

She had set a laundry system in place. Normally, he would strip off his clothes, leave them somewhere along the route to the bathroom and then ignore the pile until he ran out of clothes to wear.

"The white basket in the closet is for towels, the blue basket is for underwear and socks, and the green basket is for jeans and T-shirts."

Archer separated his clothing and headed back to the living room. He took out his pocketknife, something he always had on him no matter what, and started to open the boxes.

"Oh!" Vicky clapped her hands. "It's perfect!"

Archer pulled out a lamp for the end table by the couch. The base was a rustic bronze sculpture of a cowboy riding a horse while leading a second horse.

He unwrapped the shade and base and then Vicky handed him a bulb she had purchased at the feed store. Archer set it on the table, plugged it in, and then turned on the lamp.

"Do you like it?"

He put his arm around her shoulder, pulled her in a bit, and kissed her on the top of her head. "I love it. Thank you."

One after another, the boxes were opened, and each box held something to add to the homey look of the cabin. After all the boxes but one had been opened, Archer cut the tape on the final box and said to Vicky, "Do you mind unpacking this one while I break these boxes down?"

"Sure." She opened the box and looked inside. "I didn't order this."

"What is it?"

"Shoes. I think. Did you order these?"

"I don't know. Sometimes I hit that buy button without really thinking it through."

She raised her hand. "Guilty."

"Open them up and see."

Vicky took out the footwear box, opened it and then the smile came. Her pretty blue eyes lit up and her smile was infectious.

"Sunflower rubber boots!" She pulled them out of the box. Black calf-length rubber boots with varying sizes of sunflowers.

"Try 'em on for size," he said.

"Try and stop me!" Vicky took her boots and sat down on the couch.

One by one, she pulled on her new boots, stood up and then marched around the living room.

"What's the verdict?"

Vicky struck a pose, hands on her hips, chin lifted to show her profile, proudly wearing her new boots.

"They are perfect!" She came over to give him a hug.

"I'm glad that you like them."

Vicky put her hands on his cheeks, raised up on tiptoes, and kissed him on the lips. "I love them, Archer. I love them. Thank you."

"What are we doing here?" Cassie had agreed to meet her at a local used-car dealership. "And why are you wearing sunflower rubber boots?"

Vicky smiled and hugged her bestie. "Archer got them for me."

"Oh, he did, did he?"

"I love them."

"I see what's happening here."

"I'm not turning country," Vicky said. "I'm just adapting to my current location."

"Well, you look as happy as the cat who got the cream," Cassie said. "That's all that matters to me."

Her friend leaned down, said hi to Riley, and then asked again, "What are we doing here?"

"Well," Vicky said rather slowly, "I've been thinking that perhaps I should trade in my car and buy a truck."

Cassie did a double take. "Victoria Woodson! What in the world is happening here? You love your car!"

"I know. But I like to be higher off the ground now and I need a truck bed to haul manure."

"Did you say *manure*?"

A salesman greeted them and stopped that thread of their conversation. "What can I help you ladies with today?"

"I'd like to look at some of your trucks," Vicky said.

"I would be happy to show you around. We have a lot of low-mileage, gently used trucks."

As they walked over to the trucks, Cassie still seemed thrown for a loop. This change in vehicle was completely out of character, but the one thing Vicky and Cassie always did was let the other friend grow. Even if the "growth" was in an unexpected direction.

"So, are you a RAM girl? Ford? Chevy?"

Before she could answer, Cassie said, "She's a 'never truck' kind of girl."

Vicky laughed. "That's true."

"Wait a minute," the salesperson said. "You're Vicky Woodson. I mean Vicky Callahan."

"Yes."

"You've figured out a truck is a necessity on the ranch, right?"

"Yes. I have." Of course, she didn't add that she may not be living on Callahan Canyon for very long, because that would have broken the public image Archer and she had so carefully cultivated.

The salesman showed her all of the trucks on the lot, and she was drawn time and time again to a smaller version of Archer's truck.

"Do you want to give it a test drive?" the salesperson asked her.

"Not today," she said. "But I would like to know what the trade-in value of my SUV would be and maybe see what I'd need to qualify. Credit score. Down payment. Loan percentage rate."

"That's fine. That's fine," the salesperson said. "I'll hand you off to our finance wizard and we're here for you when you're ready."

He handed her his business card and then added, "And congratulations on your marriage and baby, Mrs. Callahan."

That's how it was. People seemed to really approve of her match with Archer. Little by little, she was feeling safe to poke out of her shell. That didn't mean that her past in Tenacity was scrubbed away. But it seemed that the town was considering moving on with her as a wife and a mother, not just the teen who made a horrible decision so many years ago. It was beginning to feel like the fresh start she had wanted, but the fresh start was in Tenacity. In large part, she had Archer Callahan to thank for showing her that she could have a better future in Tenacity, given time. And, let's face it, she thought with a smile, everyone loved babies. No matter what happened, she would love Archer to the end of her days for this priceless gift he had given to both of them. Riley and her.

Chapter Fourteen

"Vic!" Cassie had followed her to the ranch from the car lot. "This is incredible!"

"Thank you." Vicky looked around the cabin. Every space had a touch of her hand on it. "I'm proud of it."

Cassie sat down on the new couch, ran her hands over the fabric. "This is a home now."

"Can I get you something?"

"Iced tea would be good."

Vicky took a pitcher out of the fridge, poured two glasses and held out one to her bestie. "Decaf, fresh-brewed by the sun."

"You are really settling in here, Vic!"

She had to smile. As much as she had fought against the idea of ranch life—and she did know that she was still in the honeymoon phase—Vicky had found happiness in decorating the cabin, always heightened by the surprised look on Archer's face when he came home to another layer of decorating.

"I'll show you the greenhouse next." Vicky took a sip of the tea. "It was almost a goner, but with Archer's help, I've really gotten it back into working shape."

"Hence the manure."

Vicky laughed. "Hence the manure."

They caught up on their goings-on, but there was something that Vicky wanted advice on.

"I knew Archer was a good guy because he's like a blond

clone of Graham. But I had no idea that he was *this* good. He's really doing his darnedest to make me feel at home here."

"Why do I feel like there's a 'but' coming?" Cassie asked, studying her friend's face.

"But I don't know where I stand with him," Vicky said.

"Meaning?"

"He's so…" She paused, trying to find the right word. "Standoffish."

"What do you mean?"

"He hugs me, but it's a friend-zone hug for sure," Vicky explained. "He only kisses me in public. I've had to come out here several times to get him to come back to bed."

"Oh." Cassie frowned as she lifted her eyebrows suggestively. "So, no more…?"

"No." Vicky shook her head. "Total dry spell."

They had made love the last night of their honeymoon but that was the one and only time.

"I thought it went well," Vicky said. "He seemed…satisfied."

Cassie turned her body to face her, sitting cross-legged. "That's so weird. But maybe he thinks you're being standoffish."

"That's true. It makes me wonder if he isn't—"

Cassie waved her hand. "No. Don't even say it. There is no chance that he isn't attracted to you."

"I'm much bigger."

"Vic! No! Stop!" Cassie pleaded. "I can't listen to you put this on you."

"Okay," she agreed. "I won't."

"Thank you."

Vicky had wanted to ask Cassie something, but there were many hidden land mines, and she didn't want to ever seem like she was forcing Cassie into divided loyalties.

"What?" Cassie asked. "I know that look. What do you want to ask?"

"Um..." Vicky started hesitantly. "Has Graham mentioned anything?"

"About you and Archer?"

Vicky nodded.

Cassie leaned forward, put her hand on her arm reassuringly. "No. Nothing at all negative. Just that you're fixing up the place and like to grow things."

Vicky was both disappointed and relieved. Her husband was still very much a mystery. Perhaps Archer was as confused about their relationship as she was.

After she showed Cassie her greenhouse, her friend prepared to leave. But she had one last thing to share with Cassie.

"So, I've decided to put you out of your misery and have a gender reveal party."

Cassie froze, her mouth wide-open, her eyes wide and not blinking.

"Can you still hear me, Cass?"

Her friend made a tiny high-pitched sound as she grabbed a hold of her and held her too tightly.

"You won't regret this," her friend swore. "I promise you."

"Archer wants to know," she confided. "He's been just as determined as you."

"God bless, Archer Callahan." And with that sentiment, Cassie took flight, and as she backed up, Vicky could hear her friend starting to record a to-do list on her phone.

After that decision was made, Vicky felt calm. Peaceful, as she watered her newly planted vegetables and herbs. Archer had said he would bring water to the greenhouse and, as good as his word, he had done just that. Once all of the plants had been watered, she went into the cabin and sat on a wooden chair she'd found in the small room that was to be the nursery. She had looked online at many cribs and basinets and all things baby, but she hadn't really landed on the items she wanted to purchase. Perhaps it was easy to pick things out for Archer's home because it *was* his home. And, perhaps, it was difficult for her to outfit the nursery because she felt like it *wasn't* her home. On the surface, it was. She was Archer's wife; she lived with her husband. But there wasn't any evidence she could hold on to that would give her the impression that Archer had fallen in love with her or intended for the marriage to continue after her place in the community was certain.

Feeling frustrated, Vicky went into the kitchen for a cold drink and then decided to take a quick nap. The minute she closed her eyes, she fell asleep. Ranch life, however small of a taste she had taken, could tucker a person out. Especially a person who was carrying around a baby.

When she felt Archer's hand on her shoulder, she opened her eyes, not sure how long she had been asleep.

"Vic?"

"Hmm?"

"I've got a surprise."

She blinked against the late-afternoon light coming through the window, and asked, "What time is it?"

"Almost four."

She pushed herself up, checked her phone to see several texts and emails.

"How long have you been out?"

"A couple of hours," she said. "Thank you for getting the water to the greenhouse."

"Of course."

Vicky scooted to the edge of the bed and Archer reached out for her hand.

"Thank you," she said. "I need to make a pit stop. Baby on the bladder. TMI."

"I'll be on the porch."

Vicky took care of business and then joined Archer, who was sitting on the step. He had a rather playful expression on his face.

"So, do you remember our bet?"

She frowned, thought, and shook her head. "Baby brain is a real thing. I promise you."

"Horses." He gave her a clue. "If I won, I'd get another date."

She snapped her fingers and pointed at him. "And if I lost, you would help me move to Bronco."

Then she added, "But that bet is null and void because you moved me here. And we did have a second date. It was our wedding."

He laughed, rubbed his hand behind his neck and then said, "Well, I still want to cure you of that fear of horses you have."

"No," she said emphatically. "Not right now. I'm too pregnant to be messing with horses. They are too big. They are flight animals. No means no."

Archer crossed his arms in front of his body. "I hear you. I do. Just close your eyes and let me see if I can change your mind."

With her eyes closed, she said, "If it has anything to do with getting within fifty yards of a horse, I will not budge."

"Just hold your horses," he said with good humor.

"Nice one, cowboy. I saw what you did there."

"Keep those eyes closed!"

Vicky kept her eyes closed, feeling rather impatient. It was still hot and her back ached. She needed a massage, not an encounter with a horse.

"Okay," Archer called out to her. "Open your eyes."

Vicky opened her eyes and focused on Archer, and then her internal dialogue of negativity for whatever Archer had in store for her did a one-eighty. She stood up to get a closer look.

"Who is this?"

"Jasmine. Do you like her?"

Vicky took the steps carefully, holding on to the railing, her eyes trained on the miniature horse standing next to Archer, decked out in a bedazzled hot-pink halter, matching lead rope, and the fluffiest blond mane and tail Vicky had ever seen. *Like her?* Honestly, it was love at first sight.

"Seriously. She can*not* be real."

"Oh, she's real," Archer said.

Vicky stopped about ten feet away and simply stared at the miniature horse that, save for the times the horse swished her tail, absolutely could have been mistaken for a stuffed toy. The golden mini only came up to Archer's knees.

"Should I pet her?" she asked.

"If you feel safe, you surely can."

Vicky took an internal temperature of her feelings, and she didn't feel one single bit of fear or caution.

"Hi." Vicky reached out to pet the horse's golden coat. "You are a sweetheart, aren't you, Jasmine?"

"She surely is that," Archer said. "She's been in the family since I was four or five, I believe."

"My word, Jasmine." She brushed her hand over the thick mane. "You're almost as old as I am. How old is she in horse years?"

"I reckon about eighty-five or so," Archer said. "She's got arthritis and most of her teeth had to be pulled, but she's still got a lot of love to give."

"Of course you do, sweet girl." Vicky felt overwhelmed with just *love* for this little horse.

"Horses are herd animals by nature," Archer explained. "So, they aren't keen to be alone. Jasmine lost her pasture mate not too long back. They'd been together for twenty years. She's still sad about it."

"Oh, you poor baby." Vicky held her hand out, palm up, for Jasmine to sniff. "Of course you're still sad. And she can't be with the other horses?"

"No. She's the only mini on the ranch." Archer sat on a porch step, leading Jasmine with him. "Sit down with us."

Vicky sat next to Archer, feeling a kinship with the tiny, lonely horse.

"Do you see that licking and chewing she's doing? That means she feels relaxed with you."

"Well," Vicky said, an emotional waver in her voice, "that's because I feel comfortable with her."

Archer had a pleased half smile on his face when he asked, "Did I win the bet?"

She bumped his shoulder with hers and rolled her eyes. "Yes, Callahan. You won the bet. Is that what you wanted to hear?"

"Heck, yeah. I don't like to lose."

"Neither do I," she said. "But this time, I'm okay with it."

It was hard to believe, but she had made friends with a horse.

"She'll stick with you, now that you have bonded with her. It's called linking up."

"I can just take the lead rope off?"

He nodded. "Go on ahead."

She unsnapped the lead rope from the halter and then took a couple of steps forward. And darn it if Jasmine didn't follow right behind her. All around the clearing, Vicky walked while Jasmine followed. When she stopped, Jasmine stopped. When she started to walk, Jasmine started to walk.

"Where will she stay tonight?" Vicky asked. Now that she knew Jasmine, and understood how painful loneliness could be, she wanted to keep her by her side.

"She can stay here, if you want?"

"I do," she said. "But doesn't she still need other horses? Even if she has me?"

"She does. But, let's get her settled and then we will look out for a mini partner for her."

"Maybe a silver fox?" she asked. "An older man with life experience?"

"Sure." He smiled at her. "For now, I can make her a spot

under the carport. I don't use it. I'll bring back some hay, feed, bedding."

Vicky walked to where Archer was standing, with Jasmine in tow, and hugged him tightly.

"Thank you, Archer. You are always finding ways to make me happy."

Her husband looked down at her and she thought for a split second that he wanted to kiss her. But he pulled away, and then she pulled away.

"I've got to get back to work. Do you want her to stay with you?"

"Yes. I do."

Archer retrieved a large bucket for water and then headed back to his work on the ranch. Sitting on the step again, Vicky said to Jasmine as she brushed her blond mane, "He thinks that he's the one who won the bet. But we know better, don't we? We won because we have each other now, don't we?"

Jasmine must have approved of the idea because she started licking her arm.

Archer was driving Vicky to Castillo's. He had won the bet and now he was collecting. She had been working so hard to adapt to life on the ranch, he understood how isolated the cabin could feel even after working her shift at Nothin' New. The only life forms hanging out at the cabin were plants and animals. Greenhouse and Jasmine.

"Here we are." Archer parked in the lot behind the restaurant.

"Not too crowded," she noted.

"Better for us."

He jogged around the truck to open her door and help her out, then he offered his wife his arm and together they walked to the restaurant.

"Hello!" Pablo was at the door when they arrived. "Happy to see you!"

"Thank you," Vicky said. "Good to be seen."

"We are having so many specials tonight for you to try." Pablo pushed open the door to the restaurant and Vicky stepped in first.

"Surprise!"

Everyone from the wedding was in Castillo's, waiting for Vicky to arrive.

Vicky put her hand over her mouth. She looked at him and then looked at Cassie, who was walking up to her.

She turned back to Archer and asked, "Callahan? What have you done?"

"Not me," Archer said, nodding to Cassie. "She's the mastermind here."

"It's your surprise gender reveal party!" Cassie said with dramatic flair. "I couldn't have done it without Archer."

"Cassie." Vicky hugged her friend so tightly. "You are the best friend any woman could have."

"That's how I feel about you," her friend said. "Were you surprised?"

"Yes."

On Archer's arm, Vicky walked down the center aisle of the restaurant, greeting her mother, her father, her brother, Sage and May Bell. Of course, Archer's family were also in attendance.

"Welcome," Yolanda Castillo greeted her. "You had your first date here, your wedding here, and now your gender reveal. You are family now."

Vicky turned to find Archer, held out her hand for him to take. The look on her face—a combination of surprise and sheer happiness—was worth the effort he and Cassie had put into the party. Hand-in-glove, the two of them had worked to keep the secret.

Vicky had her other hand on her heart, shaking her head in disbelief.

Archer and Vicky joined Graham and Cassie in one of the last booths closest to the bar.

"I am still floored," Vicky said to them. "How did you do all of this without me knowing?"

Archer and Cassie gave each other a fist bump.

"Teamwork makes the dream work," Archer said.

"And this is your dream? Giving me a baby shower?"

Archer wondered if the love he had for the pretty Miss Woodson, now Mrs. Callahan, was easily readable on his face. When he looked into her blue eyes, he felt something so deep, so profound, so life-altering, but he still didn't know how she felt about him.

"One of them," he said simply.

The food was presented and all of Vicky's favorites were on the menu. Tacos, enchiladas, and quesadillas.

"Tonight, I am going to eat as if I don't have to watch my weight!" Vicky held up her fork with this declaration.

Archer had never known this feeling he had for Vicky. Her happiness was truly his happiness. He did all he could to make her feel at home on the ranch and he worked double-time to see her smile. To hear her infectious laugh. He wished he could be certain that there was a chance Vicky returned the depth of his feelings, but he just couldn't be sure. If not, he would let her go without a fight. It was more important to him that she was happy. And if that meant ending their marriage, he would honor her wishes. It would hurt like hell. It would hurt like nothing he'd ever felt before, not even with the first woman he had ever loved. Of course, he couldn't imagine the kind of pain heartbreak could bring to his door.

"Don't let me eat one more thing, Archer. Not one more thing!"

"They made flan for you and all of your guests," he told her.

"Okay, then," Vicky said. "Don't let me eat anything after I eat flan!"

Happily, Vicky leaned her head on his shoulder, and he welcomed the attention. She bowed into his body and said, "Other than finding out about Riley, this is the biggest surprise of my life."

"I'm glad, Vic. You deserve it."

"Don't get too comfy, lovebirds," Cassie said. "The night's not over!"

Vicky was still in a daze. The events of the evening were swirling around in her head, and she felt so blessed. Before going on that fateful date with Archer, she had been resolved to go it alone with Riley. Move to Bronco, give birth, and raise her son or daughter to the best of her ability as a single mom. And, because Riley had been a top-secret stowaway, the idea of a baby shower was impossible. Until now. Until this night.

Cassie scooted out of the booth, whistled loudly, and got the attention of the attendees.

"It's time for the main event!" Her best friend took her hand. "To the bar!"

"You don't hear that too often," Graham joked.

Vicky turned to her husband as they followed Cassie. "Did you see all of the gifts on that table? I wasn't expecting gifts. We haven't even opened the ones from our wedding yet."

He put his arm around her shoulder and she leaned into him. "What can I say? Folks love a baby and quite obviously, folks love you, too."

On Archer's arm, Vicky went into the bar that had been turned into a gift station. There was a huge piñata shaped like a baby bottle.

"I can't believe it." Vicky laughed happily, feeling like the luckiest woman. How could this be all for her? She turned back to her friends and family. "Thank you so much. I couldn't have imagined all of this. Thank you."

Cassie, comfortable in the role of organizer-slash-despot,

said, "First you will open the gifts. And then, you'll beat up that piñata."

Vicky said to everyone, "I can't thank all of you enough. You being here to celebrate this baby is better than any gift you could have bought for me."

Brent called out, "Don't judge until you see those gifts!"

The attendees laughed and then urged her on to start. One after another, Vicky opened the gifts. In those boxes were her top wish list items that she had shared with Cassie. The stroller, the car seat, the bassinet, the crib. May Bell had made a quilt just for Riley. It was so special. A treasure. Then, Archer's family gifted them a silver rattle that Archer's mother had kept from when he was a baby. His mother had clearly gone to great lengths to preserve the rattle before she passed away, so it was the only gift Vicky knew she couldn't keep. Not that one. That rattle must be saved for Archer and his wife-for-real, not convenience, and their first child together. She wouldn't do that tonight, but it had to be done.

By the time she had opened every single present, she felt so overwhelmed that her heart was near bursting with happiness. Lately, she had been feeling that she had turned a corner that led to her future and left behind her troubled past. Tonight was her graduation party. This was all about her friends and family celebrating the wonderful life she was about to bring into this world. And now she knew, in her soul, that Riley would be loved, accepted, and cared for by everyone who stood here today.

It had been such an emotional night already and then Cassie handed her a stick. "You have to start whacking at it and when you open it, it will either be blue or pink."

Everybody was cheering her on as she hit that rather tough baby bottle.

"Would you take over?" she asked Archer, handing him the stick.

"It's gonna get done," he warned her. "One whack and that's it."

"It's okay." She hugged him. "Do your thing."

Archer took that stick and in one hard hit, the baby bottle opened and pink candy fell to the ground.

Vicky had tears in her eyes as she saw all of that pink coming down. Her hand on her baby bump, she said to no one in particular. "You are blessed, Vicky. So blessed."

Archer, always acting as the proud father, put his arm around Vicky and yelled so loudly that she didn't doubt people heard him two doors down. "It's Riley Cassandra Woodson-Callahan! We are having a girl!"

Softly, and only for Vicky to hear, he said, "She'll be our little girl."

Chapter Fifteen

The week following the baby shower were the best days of Vicky's life. Now that they knew Riley was a precious little princess, the nursery was coming together. Not only had Archer been helping her put together furniture, he was also helping her pick out paint colors and basically pulling dad-to-be duty. The townsfolk of Tenacity had grown accustomed to seeing them together in town, holding hands, giving each other quick kisses. Day by day, with Archer at her side, the black cloud of the scandal had been replaced with clear blue cloudless skies.

After having lunch at the Silver Spur Café, they decided to stroll along Central Avenue. Along the way, they passed the used-car dealership where she had looked at trucks with Cassie.

"Why don't we check out some trucks?" Archer asked with a deadpan expression. And that's when she knew that Archer, somehow, had found out about her preliminary shopping for a cowgirl truck.

"It's hard to keep your personal business private in this town," Vicky complained. "Who told you?"

"I've been sworn to secrecy."

"Don't gloat," she said, pointing a warning finger at him.

Small smirk on his handsome face. "I'm not."

"Yes, you are and you need to quit it."

"Can I just say it?"

"No."

"From the very beginning—"

"Oh, lord."

"—I have said—"

"You are so annoying."

"—that there is a ranch girl in you just kicking down barn doors to get out."

She grabbed his arm playfully and said, "Stop and let me explain my reasoning."

"Go."

"Well, you know about my plants in the greenhouse."

He nodded. "I do have a vague recollection, yes."

"They need fertilizer, and fertilizer is expensive."

"True."

"And some of the best fertilizer is Black Kow." At his nod, she continued, "I bought it and put in my SUV—"

"Not advisable."

"No. Especially when one is pregnant with a hypersensitive sense of smell," she agreed. "My SUV still smells."

They continued their stroll while Archer listened to her reasoning. "Also, I live on a ranch. And that ranch has a ton of cows."

"And a very large supply of cow manure."

"My point, exactly," Vicky said. "So, that doesn't make me a cowgirl. That makes me a smart shopper. Why should I buy fertilizer from random cows when I could make my own fertilizer with cows to whom I am acquainted."

He raised an eyebrow at her. "Acquainted?"

"Okay. Not necessarily acquainted. Adjacent."

"Look," Archer said, "in all seriousness, let's take a step back and not buy a truck. I've got an ATV with a trailer hooked up to it. You can drive right out to one of the resting pastures and get as much freshly made fertilizer as you want."

Vicky looked up into Archer's face and that was the exact moment she realized that she loved her rancher husband. She knew she loved him as a friend and as the man who had helped facilitate her redemption in the town of Tenacity. And this realization that she had, along the way, actually fallen in love with her husband made her simultaneously petrified and zen. How those two feelings could occupy her mind, soul, body, and heart at the same time was a mystery. She felt vulnerable and she never allowed herself to feel that way. If only she could understand where Archer's head was at. Yes, he had been an incredible friend and once-only lover with five-star reviews from her. In fact, she wanted to be a repeat customer, but Archer still didn't seem interested. He didn't kiss her or hold her or flirt with her when they were alone, only in public. That was enough to make Vicky determined to keep her guard up, keep her true feelings to herself.

Archer quit work early to grab one of the all-terrain vehicles to teach Vicky how to drive it. Once she realized how easy it was to maneuver, new horizons would appear on the ranch. So far, they had begun taking evening walks, until the bugs drove them back to the cabin. The uneven ground was littered with rocks and sticks and he'd often thought to grab her hand and hold it, but he always held himself back. Still, it was promising that Vicky was beginning to make a life for herself on the ranch—decorating the cabin with his aesthetic while adding touches for herself. She had rehabbed the old greenhouse, long forgotten and gone to ground. Now it was a place where life grew. Jasmine had also been a big boost to Vicky's happiness. Archer had often come home to find Vicky brushing Jasmine's mane and tail, grooming her regularly, picking out the mini's tiny hooves. It seemed everywhere Vicky went, Jasmine followed.

"Vic!" Archer pulled up to the cabin and beeped the horn.

Vicky came out, wearing jeans, a T-shirt, her sunflower rubber boots, her hair pulled up into a ponytail, and a baseball cap that read Mad about Minis. She had changed—the bohemian free spirit was still there, but she had broadened the scope of what it meant to be Vicky.

"Come on, cowgirl!" He waved his hand. "Let's go get some manure."

Vicky was in good spirits, a smile on her pretty face. He loved that smile. Just as he knew, without any doubt, that he loved Vicky. He loved her enough to let her go if this life wasn't for her. But he hadn't given up hope. His marital success may just ride on Vicky happily composting manure for her greenhouse.

Vicky came around to the driver's seat and squeezed her belly behind the wheel.

"Riley and I just made it!" Vicky laughed. "What next?"

"Have you ever driven a stick?"

"Do you know what?" she asked. "I actually have. Brent had a stick shift in high school, and he taught me."

"Okay. Good. You're ahead of the game."

Archer took her through all of the components of the utility vehicle. Headlights, engine, storage, gas, brake. He saved the best for last.

"Are you ready to see something cool?"

"Always."

Archer pushed a button and the bucket directly behind the seat began to rise.

Vicky swiveled her head around. "Stop it! Are you kidding me?"

"When you've got your manure, you can drive back here and dump it right where you want it."

The sheer joy on Vicky's face made him happy.

"Ready to test it out?" he asked her.

"I was born ready!"

In seconds, Vicky took the vehicle from zero to pedal-to-the-metal, the wind nearly blowing off his cowboy hat. She drove around the clearing, shifting easily, making a figure eight, until she stepped on the brake. The sudden stop threw him forward and then backward.

"How'd I do?" Vicky asked breathlessly. When she looked at him, she asked a different question. "Are you okay? You look a little green around the gills, Archer."

"I think you got it. Just remember, Vic, the manure isn't going anywhere. You don't have to drive at top speed to get it."

"Oh." She waved her·hand. "Toughen up, cowboy."

Luckily for him, for the rest of the way, Vicky drove slowly so Jasmine could follow behind them. Vicky was very concerned about her mini and that meant he didn't have to pray for his life while the wife was driving.

They headed to one of the resting pastures and for as far as the eye could see, Vicky had her choice of the freshest cow patties.

"No cows." Vicky got out of the vehicle.

"No." Archer explained, "We rotate pastures so we always have several pastures resting so they can recover and grow."

"Well, let's get to it." Vicky grabbed the pitchfork and went on a hunt for the premium manure.

Archer helped and while he did, he watched Vicky. He'd never seen anyone so excited about cow manure, and he'd been a rancher all his life.

"Oh!" she exclaimed to herself. "This is a really good one!"

After she had filled the trailer with manure, they headed back home, at a very slow pace to accommodate Jasmine. And this time, surrounded by the pungent odor of cow manure, he wished he had the breeze of Vicky driving like a race car driver. But no luck. Still, he had to admit that it was very impressive that his city girl had added manure-hunting cowgirl to her list of qualities.

"So, what's the plan?" he asked.

"Well, according to my research, to make the compost pile, I'll need to get some twigs or sticks for a base layer. After that, I can make a layer with the carbon materials. Straw, leaves. Last, I put the manure on top. I have to water it. Not too much. Just enough to keep it moist," she continued. "The hardest part will be turning the pile to help with the decomposition."

"I can help you with that."

"Thank you," she said sincerely. "Once a week is recommended. I also have to monitor the temperature of the pile. It needs to be hot enough to kill pathogens and weed seeds."

"How long before you have usable fertilizer?"

"About three months. But if the pile is small, it could be good to go faster."

Archer got a jolt to his heart. Three months? A woman ready to fly the nest wouldn't be starting something that took a long time to finish.

"What size are you planning for?" he asked.

"I think I should go big or go home," Vicky said. "I think this could be a good revenue stream."

This was the first he'd heard of this business she had just mentioned.

"Come again?"

"Well," Vicky explained, "why not make fertilizer and sell it in town? You have plenty of raw material needed."

"Can't deny that."

"You'd have to think of a catchy name."

"How did I get involved in this venture? I'm just hearing about it and I already have several duties!"

"I can't just come here and start a business, can I?"

"Why not?" Archer shrugged. "I promise you, there isn't a Callahan on this ranch who is going to be upset with you turning cow patties into a profit."

"Hmm. Good to know."

Anything that would keep Vicky on the ranch with him, he was going to put his full weight behind it. A start-up business to bring local compost to market seemed like a good reason for her to stay.

They pulled up to the spot Vicky had designated as her target area to start composting.

"I'm pushing the button!" she called out. Then, her eyes wide open, her smile as bright as he had ever seen it, she dumped the manure. Vicky was happy. And he felt good that he had managed to bring some happiness into her life.

"This is too cool." Vicky looked at her mound of cow patties.

Archer had a question he needed to ask and this was the time. He felt it in his bones.

"So, how are you finding ranch life?"

Vicky gave a tiny smile and pointed at him. "Don't you gloat."

He held up his hands in surrender. "I wasn't going to gloat."

"I like it," she said with a pretty blush on her rounded cheeks.

He wanted to let out a whoop and throw his hat up in the air. Instead, and with a new hope in his heart, Archer put his arm around his wife's shoulders and kissed her lovely lips.

At first Vicky held back, surprised, but then stood on her tiptoes and kissed him in return.

"Thank you, Archer."

"For what?" he asked. "For the manure or the kiss?"

"Both."

They continued to be the couple about town, doing their best to be seen, whether it was a night out at Tenacity Social Club or lunch at the Silver Spur. With Archer, Vicky felt a sustained happiness that she hadn't experienced since she was eleven years old. That was when she'd believed that her life was picture-perfect. Before she'd realized her family was a sham. Now, she could honestly say that the life she was building for herself and Riley had a solid foundation. Her baby would have the life she deserved. Being Riley's mom was the most important job Vicky would ever have.

"Are you okay?" Archer asked her as they walked from lunch in town to Nothin' New.

She suddenly felt short of breath. Archer guided her to a nearby bench, with a concerned eye.

"I'm okay," she told him. "Just some aches and pains from working on the ranch."

"I did read that the third trimester can be the hardest."

He'd been reading up on pregnancy? Archer always surprised her and delighted her.

"What are your symptoms?"

Vicky took in a deeper breath. "My back aches, my hips ache, I've got heartburn all the time, I have to pee all the time, and I'm getting Braxton-Hicks contractions."

"Are you hydrated? Sometimes Braxton-Hicks is triggered by dehydration."

She couldn't help it, she had to smile. Apparently, he'd been doing *a lot* of reading! And she loved him for it. "I'm feeling better now."

Archer saw her back to Nothin' New. She unlocked the door and turned the sign around to read Open.

"Are you sure you're okay?"

"Yes." She cradled her belly and sat down in the velvet chair. "I can sit anytime. May Bell has bottled water in back, so I'll start to hydrate."

Seemingly satisfied, Archer gave her a kiss and headed for the ranch. He had been the one to start their tradition of sitting down for lunch together as often as they could, whether at the ranch or in town. It was a sweet gesture, one of those things that made her fall head-over-heels for her sexy rancher. Why Archer had wanted to be intimate at the resort but had kept it totally platonic here in Tenacity was still a nagging thought that, at times, made her feel less-than, no matter how many times she tried to deny it in her mind.

Now? She couldn't imagine wanting to make love. What she really wanted was a soak in her tub and a massage. When the door opened and a tall, slender, fifty-something woman with flawless makeup, a Gucci bag on her arm, and her ice-blond hair cut into a sharp bob, walked in. Vicky stood up to greet her.

"Please let me know if I can help you in any way."

"Thank you. I will."

The Gucci bag did throw her off a bit. Most of their clientele didn't have designer bags casually hooked onto their arms. But, then again, some women just loved a bargain and others enjoyed the hunt of searching in secondhand stores for that hidden gem. She certainly did.

The woman took some items to the dressing room and returned with several items to purchase. "Is it okay if I leave these here while I take one last look?"

"Of course. Take your time."

Vicky was feeling worn-out, her ankles were swollen, her face looked puffy, and having to take a restroom break all of the time was making her wish that Riley would just come out already!

"I think that's all for now," the woman said with a nice smile as she returned to the counter. "May Bell always has the best stuff for the best price."

Vicky rang her up and gave her the receipt. "Do you want the hangers?"

"Yes, please."

She folded the clothing, put it neatly in a Nothin' New shopping bag and handed it to the customer.

"Thank you," Vicky said. "I hope you'll come back to see us real soon."

"I will." The woman accepted the bag, walked all the way to the door, then she turned around and walked back to the counter.

"You're Vicky Callahan, aren't you?"

Vicky sat on the stool behind the counter. "Yes. I am."

The woman gave her a side-eye as she moved her head back and forth. "I was just wondering how things are going with Archer."

Why?

Instead of snapping that one-word question, Vicky said, "Great. Thank you."

"Oh. That's good to hear. I knew his first wife and when I saw that he had married you… Well, I don't want to stir up a hornet's nest. I was merely concerned that he was marrying another damsel in distress. It's uncanny the resemblance. And she was pregnant, too. But if you're doing so well together, I guess all's well that ends well."

Vicky felt a wave of nausea rush over her. She closed her eyes, fighting to regain her composure. Finally, she asked, "His first wife?"

"Oh, no! Did I tell you something you didn't know? I am horrified. Truly horrified."

Vicky wasn't convinced that the woman was sorry or horrified. She had seen that gossipy smirk on the woman's face.

If there was one thing Vicky had learned in the past year, it was how to recover quickly. "Don't worry for one second. My husband and I chose not to poison our marriage with toxic relationships of the past. We don't look back, because we aren't going that way. Now…" She stood up. "If there's nothing else, I need to close the store."

She escorted the customer out, locked the door behind her, and then turned the sign to Closed. She dropped into the velvet chair, stunned. She couldn't think clearly; she couldn't seem to catch her breath.

A first wife? How could she not have known that? How could Archer and his family have kept it a secret? When they were at Tenacity Town Hall filling out their marriage license application—she remembered this vividly—the form asked about previous marriages, and he had said, *I've got nothing to report.* He had lied on their form.

He had lied to her.

Archer came home, concerned. He'd been texting and calling Vicky for a while, and it was radio silence. Sometimes, she took a nap after work, but she hadn't felt well earlier. When he walked into the cabin, he found Vicky sitting stock-still on the couch. Her back was rigid, her feet flat on the ground, her hands folded in her lap.

"What's going on?" he asked.

Vicky looked up at him, her eyes shuttered. "You were married before. You had a wife."

Archer looked down, shook his head. He'd wondered when some rotten second shoe would drop. No matter how hard he tried, he couldn't outrun his past.

"Yes," he admitted, understanding the likely consequences to come. "I was."

Tears began to flow down Vicky's cheeks. He'd never seen her cry before, and it was gut-wrenching.

He went to the couch, knelt down before her, tried to take her hand in his. But she pushed his hand away.

"You *lied* to me," Vicky said. "You lied on our marriage license application!"

"No, I didn't." Archer dragged a wooden chair over to where his wife was sitting so they could hash this out. His gut was twisted into a knot, his heart was pounding; he was jittery with adrenaline. His first wife, Marina, was still haunting him years later. He dropped his head into his hands before he lifted his head and brushed his hair back from his face. This could be the thing that ended his marriage. Hadn't he paid enough for that mistake? Would he ever be free of her?

"Her name was Marina. That marriage was annulled. It never

happened. And because it never happened legally, I didn't have to put it on the form."

"Okay." Vicky shot back. "But that doesn't mean you shouldn't have told me! I asked you if you had anything to tell me and you said *no*!"

Archer could see the writing on the wall. He couldn't think of one thing he could say to change the direction of this conversation. All he could do was tell the truth, and hope Vicky could believe him.

Archer dropped his eyes down with a drawn-out sigh. He ran his hand over his head several times before he looked up at Vicky.

"I didn't tell you about it because I don't want to talk about it. I don't want to think about it. I wasn't looking at my past when we were filling out that application, Vic, I was looking at a future I may have with you.

"Who told you about this?" he asked. "No one in Tenacity knows about this, other than my family."

"A woman came into the shop. She didn't look like a customer. Designer everything. She had an accent. Russian maybe? She told me—not that it matters."

"That's Polina," he said bitterly. "Marina's mother. Why can't she just leave well enough alone?"

Vicky rose with her car keys in hand. "I'm leaving, Archer."

He stood up but couldn't bring himself to beg her to stay.

Vicky walked past him on the way to the door, opened it, grabbed her favorite, most delicate plant, and walked down the steps. He saw that there was a suitcase already in the back of her SUV.

Jasmine saw Vicky and cantered over to her. Vicky sat on the step, hugged Jasmine and started to cry again. "I'm so sorry, Jasmine. If I could take you with me, I would. I love you."

The mini horse whickered at her, but it wasn't enough to stop Vicky from getting in behind the wheel and starting the engine. Before she could pull away, Archer walked over to her car and tapped on the window. She rolled it down.

"What the heck now, Vic? Are you leaving me? Are you leaving the life we have built here?"

He just couldn't bring himself to enter the word *divorce* into a conversation that was already fraught with emotion.

"I don't know, Archer. You need to give me some space."

And with that said between them, Vicky drove away, taking a piece of his heart with her.

Chapter Sixteen

"What happened?"

"I left Archer." The minute she returned to her apartment above Tenacity Grocery, Vicky threw herself down on her love seat and called Cassie. From the sound of her voice, her friend knew immediately something was wrong. "Archer was married before."

Her friend was silent for a second or two before Vicky heard Cassie ask Graham, "Archer was married before?"

Then came another pause. She heard Graham's deep voice in the background ask, "Who the heck dredged *that* up?"

"So, that's a yes," Cassie said and then asked, "Why is this the first I'm hearing about it?"

"Cass. Cass," Vicky said in a raspy, tired voice. "I don't want this to cause problems for Graham and you. I don't want your relationship to be collateral damage."

"It won't, Vic. Don't worry about that. Do you need me to come over?"

"No. Some things just can't be fixed with mint-chocolate-chip."

After she hung up with Cassie, she put her fiddle-leaf fig plant back in its original spot. It was finicky and could be thrown out of balance for any number of reasons.

"Well, my Western African beauty," Vicky crooned to the plant. "There's no place like home."

But the truth was, the apartment was tiny and no longer felt like home. It was a shell, devoid of life. The furniture looked shabby, not chic. There wasn't any elbow room. No greenhouse. No miniature horse. No compost project. Most importantly, there was no Archer. Despite her best efforts, she'd become deeply attached to her husband and the ranch.

"Okay, Riley," she said as she cradled her belly. "We can tackle anything together. Just you and me, kid. Strong, capable, badass women."

She had only packed her toiletries, her favorite nighty, and some undergarments. It was a quick pack, during duress, so eventually, once she had time to rest her brain and think this bombshell through, she'd have to figure out her next steps. In her life, she had faced adversity, and as it turned out, it had prepared her for a moment like this. Of course, she wanted her marriage to work. She loved Archer. She was in love with Archer. But her main question remained: Was she just another damsel in distress for Archer to swoop in and fix? She had told him frequently that she did not need to be rescued, and she resented the townsfolk who pitied her. To find out that she might actually be married to someone who pitied her was devastating. Devastating!

She changed into her nighty, crawled into her full-sized bed. The pillows seemed flat and uncomfortable, the comforter was raggedy, and the mattress felt like she was sleeping on a cement block. She tossed and turned, trying to get some relief for her aching hips and sore back. Thankfully, she managed to fall into a restless sleep. Her bladder woke her up and she checked her messages. Not one was from Archer. He was respecting her boundary. It made her feel sad and lonely, and so hurt inside that she felt she might never recover. More than anything else, Archer had been her friend.

Vicky padded into the kitchen, opened the freezer and was grateful to see a gallon of ice cream. She opened it and peeked inside.

"There is a God!"

She put the nearly full mint-chocolate-chip in the microwave and fished in a drawer for a tablespoon. She took her ice cream to the love seat and listened to the sounds of the street below as people walked along the sidewalk.

Once, she had loved those sounds. Even when she was alone, it felt like she was connected. Not tonight. And perhaps never again. She had grown accustomed to the sounds of the ranch. Owls hooting at night, the wind bringing the moos of cows from the hills down to the cabin. The squirrels and the birds. Acorns dropping onto the tin roof, at first unsettling, but now rather soothing.

"I miss the sound of his voice," she told Riley. "I already miss the scent of his skin on his pillow. I miss the weight of his body next to me in the bed. And his ability to make me laugh or to not take myself so seriously."

But she couldn't just ignore the fact that she'd been blindsided by a stranger who'd told her that he'd been married before. It was like that woman had known her weakness. She did not want to be a damsel in distress for Archer to rescue. Now, she discovered, she was damsel in distress number two.

"I'm so tired." Vicky threw the empty carton in the trash and headed back to her bed. In the darkness, while she couldn't sleep, she tried to keep herself from going stir crazy and began to solve the puzzle of how to make this apartment work for her and Riley. It would be a tight squeeze, but she was determined to makc it work.

"We'll be okay," she assured Riley. But she knew that she was really trying to convince herself.

"Where've you been, brother?" Graham found him cleaning out the stall he had built for Jasmine. "We need you."

"You know where I've been and why."

Graham sighed. "Yeah. I know."

A week had gone by like a snail crossing a highway. It dragged on and on and on. He hadn't been working on the ranch. He'd been staying at the cabin, taking care of the things that Vicky loved. She loved to care for things: animals, people, plants. Now that she was gone, he felt compelled to pick up where she'd left off. He couldn't let her house plants die. He couldn't let her greenhouse vegetable plants wilt, and he couldn't let Jasmine miss her grooming.

Graham followed him into the greenhouse.

"Do you think it was your ex-mother-in-law?" his brother asked him.

"I have no doubt. Polina. Cold as an iceberg, mean as a rattlesnake." Archer started his routine of caring for the plants. "Ten years, bro. Ten years. And I get yanked right back to a time that I have been trying to erase for a decade."

Graham leaned back against the counter, scratching his stubble with his fingernails. "I know, brother. I thought we were done with all of that."

Archer was still reeling. Things were just beginning to gel with Vicky. She was excited about ranch life and starting a business. Archer finished watering the plants and then whistled for Jasmine, who had been showing signs of depression.

The mini trotted over to him and let him begin to brush her mane. "I know, Jazzy Jazz. I miss her, too."

Graham had a frustrated expression on his face, and Archer just decided to ignore it.

"This isn't sustainable, Arch," his older brother said. "You've got to snap out of it. There's work to be done and you have your fair share."

Archer felt anger bubbling up inside. "You've been down on Vicky from the start."

"I was protecting you."

"I love her, Graham." Archer rose up to face his brother. "I *love* her. Way before our first date, I knew. But I couldn't trust it. I couldn't move past what I'd been through. And it cost me my marriage."

Archer couldn't find any more words to say. "I'll catch you later, Graham. You'll know I'm ready to get back to work when you see me."

Archer climbed the porch steps, took off his boots, then walked through the door and into the world that Vicky had created. He grabbed a beer out of the fridge and sat down on the couch.

"I miss you, Vic. I surely do miss you."

He had grabbed his phone what felt like a hundred times to call his wife, to text his wife. But one thing he had learned about Vicky was that when she said she needed space, it was best to give her space. So, counter to what he wanted to do, he respected her wishes.

He tossed the empty bottle into the trash and went into the nursery. They had worked so hard on this space, and they had bonded over it. They had picked the shade of green on the walls, which he'd painted. The dinosaur appliqués were the perfect tie to Tenacity's claim to fame. The crib would grow with Riley, eventually turning into her first big-girl bed. Organic sheets, a closet full of baby clothing. A mobile of the planets that was a nod to his interest in the universe.

He wasn't just losing Vicky. He was losing his daughter. Louis was the biological father, but Archer was Riley's real dad, her father of the heart. And he had fallen in love with her, even before he'd known her name, just as easily and just as quickly as he had fallen in love with her mother.

Archer pinched the corners of his eyes. Tears had formed. But he had to beat them back. Was there hope of a reconciliation? No matter how many times he mulled it over, he just couldn't figure it out. All he could do was wait for Vicky to contact him. When that call or text came, would it be to see if they could work things out or would it be a call to move her out of his cabin and back into her apartment?

"Damned if I know."

"Hi, May Bell."

Vicky was relieved that her boss had returned from visiting her sister in Des Moines, Iowa.

"Let me get a good look at you." May Bell studied her face. "You're very sad. Why are you sad, dear one?"

Vicky didn't want to cry anymore. She had shed enough tears.

"Archer and I—" She stopped then restarted. "I've left him."

Now May Bell looked concerned as she processed the unexpected news.

"No. No, no, no, no, no." Her boss shook her head slowly. "No."

"I'm afraid so." Vicky slumped down into the velvet chair. "Other than Cassie, I haven't told anyone. Yes, I've had some curious looks when I come and go from the apartment, but I don't think the gossip mill has seized onto it. Only a matter of time."

May Bell thought with narrowed eyes. "And I've been out of town, so I'm not plugged into the mill. Tell me what happened."

For hopefully the last time, Vicky told May Bell the story of the woman with a big-city vibe who'd come into Nothin' New to, from her perspective, tear her marriage asunder.

"Oh! I'm madder than a wet hen. To use my shop for evildoing. I will need to sage later. But for now, do not let that woman win, Victoria! Don't let her ruin your marriage. For me, precious. Don't turn your back on Archer. He's got a heart of gold, that one."

Vicky went back to her apartment and closed all of the curtains. Why was she always caught up in one secret after another? She kept the secret of the stolen money for sixteen years.

A short time back, she had been hiding her pregnancy. Then she'd hidden that her marriage was a marriage of convenience. Now, she was trying to hide the fact that her marriage of convenience had ended abruptly. The hardest part was being away from Archer. Oh, how she missed him. May Bell had always given her the best advice, and this time she had told her to reconsider ending her marriage. According to May Bell, she at least owed herself and Archer that much.

An unexpected knock on the door startled her. She walked quietly over to it, looked through the peephole and groaned. She unlocked the door and opened it.

"Hi, Graham."

"Hi, Vicky."

She didn't ask him to come in.

"Can I talk to you for a minute?"

Annoyed, she breathed in, rolled her eyes and then motioned for him to enter. Graham sat down at her table. She joined him, arms crossed in front of her.

"Why are you here, Graham? You've gotten what you wanted."

Graham shook his head. "No. I didn't want this."

"Look, I'm tired—"

"Just give me a minute, Vic, okay? Archer is in a bad way. Worse than I've ever seen him." Archer's brother held up his hand to stifle her response. "It wasn't all that long ago that you—the person who was against me—came to me, and that's why I trusted you when you said Cassie loved me. You wouldn't have said that if it weren't true."

She couldn't deny the facts of his case. It hurt her to know that Archer was in pain. Vicky would never want that for him, no matter what happened between them.

"What are you trying to say, Graham? Archer loves me?"

"Yes. That's exactly what I'm here to say."

"I remember right before we left for our honeymoon, you told me that Archer couldn't resist helping birds with broken wings."

"I'm sorry I said that."

"But you did," she said. "You meant Marina and you meant me. Right? Two birds with broken wings who needed to be rescued."

Graham looked as frustrated as she felt when he continued. "I know this looks bad on Archer, that he didn't tell you. But no one in the family talks about this. He was twenty, his first time living off the ranch while training to be a farrier. He met a young lady, and he really cared for her. She was in a rough spot with her family and then she told him she was pregnant. Archer did the right thing. He married her. And he was excited about being a father. Out of all of us brothers, Arch was the one who wanted to get married and have a family one day. Probably because he was so young when we lost our dad."

"What happened?" Vicky felt stunned. "Is there a child?"

Graham drummed his fingers on the tabletop. "No. There wasn't a child. There never was a child."

"Oh, no."

"Archer found out. The marriage was annulled. It's taken a long time for Archer to trust again. He trusts you. He loves you, Vic. I promise you. I wouldn't be here pleading his case otherwise."

Vicky put her hand over her mouth. All of the anger she'd used to build up a wall around her heart to keep Archer out dissipated. And the wall crumbled.

"I have to go, Graham."

Vicky grabbed her purse and her keys and shuttled Archer's brother down the stairs as quickly as she could. At her car, she turned and said, "Thank you, Graham."

"Thank you, Vicky. For loving my brother."

Archer was in the greenhouse, harvesting some tomatoes, when he heard a car pull up and a door slam shut. He walked to the doorway and halted. It was Vicky. His Vicky. He put the tomatoes on the counter, wiping his hands off on his jeans as he walked to her. The look on her face was pure love for him. He saw it. He felt it.

"You're here."

"I'm here," Vicky said. "Graham came to see me."

"Did he?"

"Yes."

"So he told you," her rancher husband said. "He's always looking out for me, even when I don't want him to."

"He did tell me. And I'm sorry, Archer. It's terrible what happened to you."

"I never thought you needed to be saved, Vic. I just needed to keep you near me. I've loved you for a very long time."

"I know that now."

Archer couldn't stand to be this close to his love and not hold her, kiss her.

"Vicky," he said around the lump in his throat, "have you come back to me?"

"Yes."

He took her face in his hands, looked into her eyes, so clear and blue. "I love you, Vicky. From the first moment I met you, when we were just kids really, I have loved you."

"I love you, Archer." His wife said the words that held the key to unlock his heart.

"I'm sorry," he said between kisses. "I should have told you."

"Maybe," Vicky said. "But I understand wanting to bury painful things."

Archer held on to Vicky's hand, not wanting to ever let go. "I didn't know if you loved me, Vicky. And that made me hide my emotions from you."

"I did, too," she admitted. "I was scared, Archer. And that fear made me send you all sorts of mixed signals. I know I did. But when you only held my hand in public, or only kissed me in public, I thought you didn't love me."

Archer took her in his arms. "I didn't want to put pressure on you, Vic. I knew if you couldn't make a life on the ranch, I'd have to love you enough to let you go."

His wife, with so much tenderness in her eyes, said, "You will never need to let me go. I love you and I love the life I'm building here."

Archer drew her back into his embrace. Kissing her face, her neck and her lips. She smelled so sweet, and his humble cabin had felt so empty without her.

"Oh!" Vicky exclaimed.

"What?"

"Riley is kicking the heck out of me!"

Archer smiled for the first time in over a week. "Riley is going to enter the world looking for her cowgirl boots."

"I've accepted it." Vicky smiled. "I'm a cowgirl and Riley will be a cowgirl, too."

Vicky then looked around. "Speaking of cowgirls. Where's my horse?"

Together, hand in hand, they walked over to the stall to visit Jasmine.

"There you are, sweet girl."

The mini stood up, nickered and came right to Vicky.

"She's missed you."

"I've missed her."

"Welcome home, Vicky," he said, his arm around her shoulders, holding her close to him.

"Thank you," she said. "It's good to be home."

Vicky slowly opened her eyes and reached for her husband. Lying on his back, arm behind his head, he was bare-chested and propped up on the pillows. For the first time since their honeymoon, they had made love.

"Did you sleep?" Vicky struggled a bit to roll over. She rested her head on Archer's chest, feeling more loved and cared for than at any other time in her life. Archer was her person, and she was his.

"A bit," he said.

She looked up at him. "I missed you."

"It was like being deprived of air when you were gone."

She kissed his neck. "We will never be apart again."

He pulled her closer and kissed her. "Never again."

Vicky's stomach growled and they both laughed.

"Let's go see what we can scrounge up," Archer said.

She slipped on his bathrobe and followed him into the kitchen. While he checked out the food situation, she checked on her plants.

"You took care of my plants."

"Yes. I did," he said. "I wanted you to see that I love them because I love you."

"Thank you." She rested her hip on the counter and peered around him into the refrigerator. "Any luck?"

Archer shut the fridge door. "Nope."

"Solution?"

Her husband shrugged one shoulder. "Castillo's?"

"I'll meet you at your tree-house truck in five minutes. Maybe ten."

Good as her word, she dressed as quickly as her third-trimester body would allow and headed out to the truck that Archer was cooling down for her. He jumped out, met her at the passenger door and helped her into her seat.

"I do love to be up high."

He winked at her. "My cowgirl."

"My cowboy."

They arrived at Castillo's with a sense of nostalgia. How far they had come from their first date. Her arm hooked onto his, she walked into the restaurant, fulfilled and looking forward to a bright future with her husband and her daughter.

Pablo greeted them warmly, happy to see them. He sat them at the same booth where they'd had their first date and where they had sat during the baby shower. They ordered their food, and then Archer reached over the table to hold her hands.

"I need to ask you something," he said.

"Okay."

"I have to tell you that I fell in love with Riley before I knew her name."

Vicky's eyes started to water.

"The first time I heard her heartbeat," Archer told her, "I was hooked."

"Thank you. For loving her. For loving me."

"The other night, it was the first time I felt her kick. I would put my arm around you at night, I could feel her move and there was a time when I swear, she pushed her hand toward mine."

Vicky couldn't seem to speak, her heart was so full. How could she have been so lucky to have Archer Callahan as her one true love? A man who had a big enough heart to embrace her child as his own.

"What I want to ask is..." Archer paused and took a breath. "Would you allow me to adopt Riley?"

For the second time in a week, she was unable to hold back her tears. Pablo walked by, saw her crying, and held out a napkin to her. "Why are you crying in Castillo's?"

She wiped away her tears. "These are happy tears, Mr. Castillo."

"Oh!" he said. "Happy tears are okay."

When Mr. Castillo left, Vicky reached out for Archer's hands. "I love you, Archer. And I can't think of anything I would love more than for you to adopt Riley. She is such a lucky girl."

"I'm the lucky one," Archer said. "My beautiful bride, I will love you for forever and a day."

"Yes, my handsome rancher," she promised. "Forever and a day."

* * * * *